THE BAREFOOT DODGERS

THE BAREFOOT DODGERS

by

Robert Hitt Neill

THE BAREFOOT DODGERS

Copyright 2001 by Robert Hitt Neill

All Rights Reserved
ISBN # 1-879034-21-2

Designed & Produced by
Mark Weilenman

Cover Photo by
Betsy Neill

Printed in the USA by Lightning Source. Published by Brownspur Books, P.O. Box 6, Stoneville, MS 38776. Library of Congress Catalog in Publication Data Pending.

Other Books by Robert Hitt Neill:
The Flaming Turkey
Going Home
The Jakes
The Voice of Jupiter Pluvius
How To Lose Your Farm In Ten Easy Lessons & Cope With It
Don't Fish Under The Dingleberry Tree
Beware The Barking Bumblebees
Outdoor Tables & Tales (compiled & edited)
The Magnolia Club (compiled & edited)

Forewarning:
Spooky Stuff

I'm not sure I wrote this book.

Oh, sure, I spent the weeks pecking away to put the words on paper, and the copyright is in my name, but....

As with most cogitative writers, the stories, plots, characters, and scenarios rattle around in my head for months, maybe even years, then suddenly jell and literally demand to be written. At that point, a creative passion consumes a writer and goes on for eight to twelve hours a day, seven days a week, for maybe a month or two. It's a real tragedy when that happens during deer or turkey season, or when your child is fixing to get married, or just as the World Series begins.

But THE BAREFOOT DODGERS didn't work thataway. Never a thought of such a plot had crossed my mind; indeed, I was working on another book and a screenplay. I was on my way to a speaking engagement in Pensacola when -- BAM! -- somewhere close to Lucedale, Mississippi, might near the whole book sprung unbidden into my head, with such force that I had to pull over and make notes before driving on -- with the notebook propped on the dash to make further barely legible jottings on. By the time I headed back from Florida (too fast!) I had most of the characters and the main plot outlined. After Thanksgiving, I wrote the main part of this in about two weeks.

The characters are to much extent modeled after real people, some of whom played for the original Barefoot Dodgers when I was a kid. One of the heroes is obviously alike Bud Granger, who grew up here on Brownspur, captained the Barefoot Dodgers when they won the state championship, and could literally bend a curveball around the corner of the haybarn -- no kidding! Bud left the place when I was in high school, to go north and seek his fortune. I had not heard from him in thirty years.

I printed out a first draft of THE BAREFOOT DODGERS and sent it to a publisher's consultant on Friday. On Sunday, guess who drove up into my driveway, unannounced?

Bud Granger. He'd retired and come home. After greetings and introductions to Betsy, my wife, we went into the kitchen where the coffee was. Know what Bud began talking about, with no prompting whatsoever from me? The Barefoot Dodgers!

Right, it's spooky.

Yes, I gave him another printout. Yes, he liked it; he should, being one of the heroes. He called a month later to say that he had also made his mother and sister read it, as well as looking up two other former Barefoot Dodgers and letting them read it. "We don't want you to change a word," he declared, "All we want to do is sit down with you and tell you some other things that happened so you can flesh out the book."

We met and talked several times, and I began a rewrite. One year later, Bud Granger had a heart attack and died.

Another hero is modeled after one of the gutsiest kids I ever coached, Mike Ethridge. He, his brother Mark, and my son Adam grew up the closest of friends. Mike was a Cystic Fibrosis victim, and I was reluctant to let him play Little League baseball on our team because of his condition. Yet his parents finally prevailed on me to let him try, and I did, fearfully.

Mike led the team in hitting that year, was team MVP, and made the All-Star Team.

We played for the league championship that summer, and Mike later managed a high school championship team, though he never was really healthy enough to play that well again.

Many times an author will run a disclaimer: "No one in this book is remotely like anyone I ever knew before, so I can't be sued for any portrayals similar to real people."

Bull. The Barefoot Dodgers were real, and good. Bud, Mike, Mark, Adam, Longmile, Uncle Eb, and others were the basis for my characters, though this is a fictional treatment of the team.

This is a story about people.

THE BAREFOOT DODGERS

is dedicated to:

The Barefoot Dodgers

And the white boys who got to practice with them:

Alton and Troy McIntire

And the next generation, who lived most of these episodes:

Adam Neill, Bryon McIntire, and Mike and Mark Ethridge

Postscript:

Jessie Ford, who taught me how to drive a tractor and now resides in Chicago, was down visiting recently, and I was telling him about this book. Jessie used to play for the Barefoot Dodgers before the team that Bud captained won the state championship and he recalled several of the players on that championship team. Weeks later he wrote me from Chicago with the line-up, as he remembered them:

Bud Granger, Captain	Longmile Harrison, Coach
Jimmy and Phil Harrison	John and Hal Hall
T.C. Boykin	Sammy and Luke Jones
Vernell and Nathanial Gordon	Teddy Woods
Joe Adams	Russell Williams
Joe Wade	Dewitt, William, and
	James Prewitt

That's right, it all happened to somebody, durn near like I wrote it. Of course, like Great-Uncle Sam Neill said, "Tis a poor piece of cloth that can stand no embroidery!"

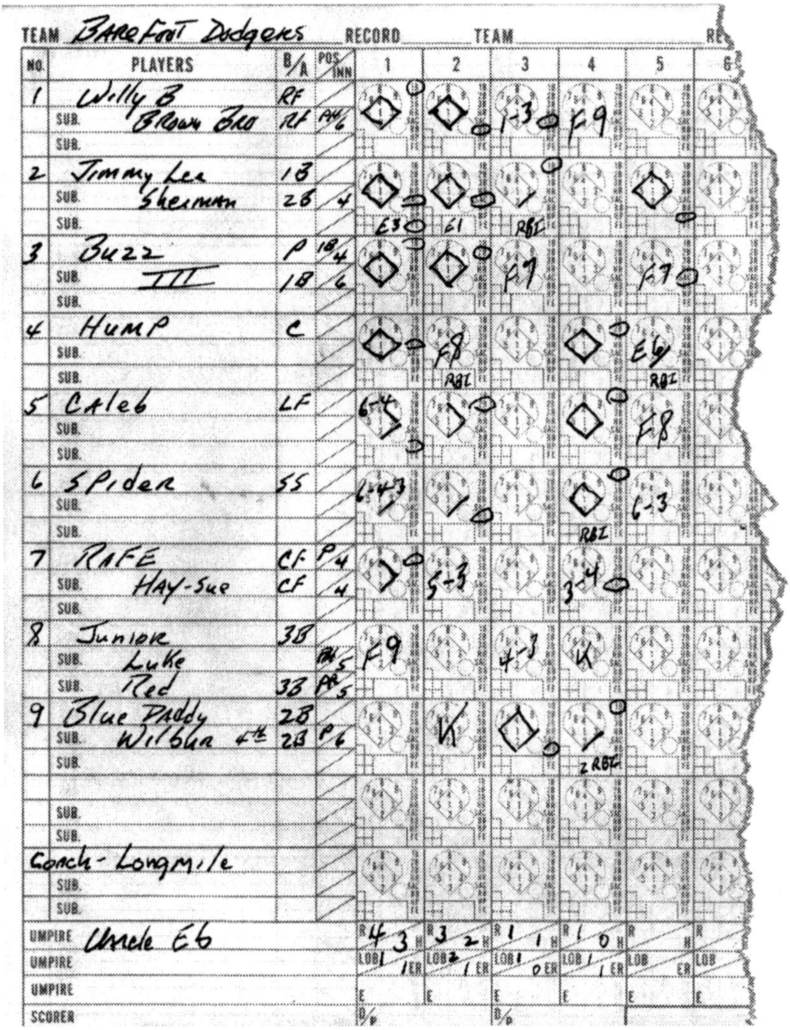
TEAM Barefoot Dodgers RECORD TEAM
NO. PLAYERS B/A POS/INN 1 2 3 4 5 6
1 Willy B RF
SUB. Brown Bro RF PH/6
2 Jimmy Lee 1B
SUB. Sherman 2B 4
3 Buzz P 1B/4
SUB. III 1B 6
4 Hump C
5 Caleb LF
6 Spider SS
7 Rafe CF P/4
SUB. Hay-Sue CF 4
8 Junior 3B
SUB. Luke PH/5
SUB. Red 3B PR/5
9 Blue Daddy 2B
SUB. Wilbur 4th 2B P/6
Coach - Longmile
UMPIRE Uncle Eb
UMPIRE
UMPIRE
SCORER

Chapter One

Buzz Waterman kicked angrily at the mound, which was simply that: a mound of dirt. He had come into the ninth inning with a seven to four lead, and now the tying run was at the plate, with no outs. Buzz glared at the batter, a shirtless, skinny kid who had already touched him for two hits today. He had bounced a good curve ball off the side of the haybarn in his last at-bat. What to throw him now?

Not that it had all been Buzz's fault. The leadoff man had lifted a high fly that Caleb would normally have eaten up in left field, but the cows had drifted back into left and Caleb had run smack into the spotted steer, turning an easy fly ball into a triple. A pooter into the hole had been backhanded by Spider Webb, who had tried to go home instead of spinning to throw to first. Hump Henderson had not been able to reach the high throw, and the batter had gone all the way to third on the play, for the ball went through the catchpen fence.

Hump was now calling for the curve, but Buzz shook him off. He wanted to start this guy off with a high tight fastball, and finally got that signal. Into the stretch, glancing back at Junior Johnson faking a move to the bag to hold the runner on third. High and tight; too tight -- the skinny kid had to bail out of the box. However, now the stage was set for the slow curve on the outside corner, which Uncle Eb called a strike. One more fastball in for strike two, then Buzz floated the knuckler up there, and Skinny went fishing for it, way out in front for the strikeout. "Way to go!" he heard Third Alexander yell from his perch on the catchpen fence.

The cleanup hitter popped up an outside curve to Spider at shortstop, but the next man fudged up in the box and rapped one down the line in right. The run scored from third, and the batter saw he had a chance for extra bases, but turned too wide rounding first. As the galloping player glanced over his shoulder to see if Willy B had run the ball down, his left foot hit a fairly fresh cow pie at the edge of the outfield grass, and he tumbled. Willy B's throw was on the money to Blue Daddy at second, and Uncle Eb easily made the "Out" call from home plate. The opposing coach rushed the elderly umpire.

"What you mean, he was out?! He slipped on that cow pie, or he'da had a triple! That's a ground rule double!" the coach screamed.

"Only a ground rule double if the **BALL** centers a pile in the outfield," Uncle Eb ruled, as even the arguing coach knew he would. "Runners and fielders take their chances with livestock and their droppin's in the outfield. Your man turned too wide and got outa the baseline. Game's over," the old man shrugged, as the fans perched on the catch pen fence cheered.

The Barefoot Dodgers had won another one!

Longmile Henderson, the Dodgers' coach, stood from his seat on the rough bench beside Luke Alexander, who kept the scorebook. "Aw right, guys, Mr. Leroy's got RC's in the Store. Git one and come on back out. We'll do a little outfield practice, if Luke don't mind hittin' some. Buzz, get some ice on that arm. Hump, don't get outa your gear," he instructed his son, "I want Rafe to chunk for a while to warm up for the second game. Third, you mind throwin' some to Caleb and Jimmy Lee in the net? They still ain't learned how to hit a curve ball." This last was directed toward a well-built, tow-headed youth sitting on the top board of the fence, who grinned and nodded assent before joining the other youngsters trooping into the plantation commissary, where his father had unlocked the drink machine for the team.

"Good game, Buzz," Leroy Alexander congratulated the winning pitcher. "That spotted steer messed up Caleb on that long fly, but it messed in the right place to get that last batter out. You better give him a little extra sweet feed tonight!" The owner of Brownspur Plantation pulled a couple of ice trays from the top of the drink machine and handed them to his namesake, Leroy Alexander III. "Pop those out into a plastic bag for Buzz, Third. And refill 'em this time."

"Yessir," the towhead replied. "Buzz, how come I can't get my knuckleball to float like that? You had ole Skinny out in front of it by six feet!"

"I'll show you again while you chunk to Caleb and Jimmy Lee," the tall lanky pitcher offered. "You gotta hold it further back in your palm, I think." Buzz Waterman drained half his cold drink in one swallow. "Thanks, Mr. Leroy," he nodded.

Outside, Third's younger brother was swinging a fungo bat. Luke Alexander was only a year younger than Third, and idolized the blonde athlete. While the tanned and fit Third competed in almost every high school sport, Luke had never been able to play anything. He had Cystic Fibrosis, a disease affecting the lungs and sweat glands. Though he had excellent hand-eye coordination, and plenty of strength, Luke could not run without endangering himself of a heat stroke and phlegm attack. His role with the plantation baseball team had been to keep score and hit fly balls to the outfield. In pickup games, Luke would sometimes be allowed to bat with designated runners, who started from behind home at the crack of his bat. Few pitchers could get a ball past his reach, and many of his runners scored. Most plantation ball fields did not have outfield fences, and unless a ball centered a pile of cow mess, home runs were simply balls hit far into the gaps or over the outfielders' heads.

The Barefoot Dodgers had been the name of the Brownspur

team for as long as anyone recalled, even back when Longmile had played and Leroy Alexander Sr. had bought the equipment. The stocky coach had been a catcher, as was his own son, and had played in the old Negro League for several years. After the major leagues had begun to integrate, Longmile had caught briefly in AAA, but a broken thumb had ended his career. He had returned to Brownspur to sharecrop and run the stands at the plantation cotton gin during the fall. Leroy Alexander Jr., who had played pasture baseball with Longmile in their youth, and who had gone on to play college football himself, had suggested that the former minor leaguer might enjoy coaching the Barefoot Dodgers, and the two had worked together to upgrade the field and equipment when the elder Alexander had passed away.

While the white boys could not play in the "official" games on Saturday and Sunday afternoons, they had grown up with all the players on the plantation, and practiced regularly with the Dodgers during the summer. Though Luke could do no more than hit with a designated runner, his southpaw sibling often pitched and played first, alternating with Buzz at these positions. The plantation shop manager's son, "Red" Wood, was a better fielder than Junior Johnson, the Dodgers' starting third baseman, but was a weak hitter. The only discrimination the team had ever experienced was when a Mexican migrant settled on Brownspur as pressman at the cotton gin. His son Jesus, called "Hey-Sue" by the other youngsters on the place, was begrudgingly allowed to participate in pasture baseball only after intervention by both coach and owner. Longmile and Mr. Leroy had insisted that Hey-Sue be included, but the youngster was never really accepted by either the whites or blacks.

"That's a strange situation," Mr. Leroy had mused to Jose Melendez at the gin one afternoon. "These white and black boys have grown up together out here as friends, and while they are aware of differences in opportunities, they aren't affected much by that at their age and stage. They get along like boys anywhere. But let a foreigner come in, and both white and black seem united against him. Yet all this race stuff we read about pits white against black."

"Ees fonny, Senor Leroy, but I think my son onderstands somehow, and ees not hurt by thees feelings. Jesus ees good kid. Eet will work out een time." The man smiled wistfully. "Senor, ees not all block en white; we browns have problem also."

The plantation owner nodded ruefully. "I see that. But you let me know how I can make it easier for Jesus."

Melendez grinned, "He say cow mess up here ees slicker than in Mexico; harder to run through. Maybe you change your cow feed to make cow mess dryer?"

Alexander laughed. "It's the humidity here, Jose. Takes a cow pie ten times longer to harden. But, hey, at least these boys are just stepping in it. When I was coming along, we played football in it too. When I'd get tackled, sometimes I'd be facedown in a cow pie!"

"Senor, I am grateful that Jesus ees only stepping in it now. But I am even more grateful that, here in America, he has a chance to play either sport at will. He would not have that choice had we remained in Mexico."

TEAM **Barefoot Dodgers**   RECORD   TEAM   R

NO.	PLAYERS	B/A	POS INN	1	2	3	4	5	6
1	Willy B	RF				1-3	F9		
	SUB. Brown Bro	RF	PH 6						
2	Jimmy Lee	1B							
	SUB. Sherman	2B	4	E3	6-1	RBI			
3	Buzz	P	1B 4			F9		F9	
	SUB. III	1B	6						
4	Hump	C			F8		E6		
	SUB.				RBI		RBI		
5	Caleb	LF		6-4			F8		
	SUB.								
6	Spider	SS		6-4-3		6-3			
	SUB.					RBI			
7	Rafe	CF P 4			5-3	3-4			
	SUB. Hay-Sue	CF	4						
8	Junior	3B		F9	4-3	4			
	SUB. Luke		PH 5						
	SUB. Red	3B	PH 5						
9	Blue Daddy	2B		K					
	SUB. Wilbur 6th	2B	P 6			2 RBI			
	SUB.								
	SUB.								
	SUB.								
Coach - Longmile									
	SUB.								
	SUB.								

UMPIRE Uncle Eb		4 3	3 2	1 1	1 0	0	
UMPIRE		LOB 1 / ER	LOB 2 / ER	LOB 1 / ER	LOB 1 / ER	LOB / ER	LOB
UMPIRE		E	E	E	E	E	E
SCORER		B/P		B/P			

Chapter Two

"LUKE, LUKE, LUKE, LUKE!" cheered the bench, emphasizing the vowel sound and drawing it out. The CF Kid, as Third sometimes called him, had just smacked his fourth homer in a row off of his brother, with Willy B coming around to score well ahead of Rafe's throw. It was a Wednesday afternoon, and the plantation youth were involved in a pickup game. The younger Alexander was batting for his whole team in the bottom of the fifth, the runners beginning from a point three steps back of the catcher. Buzz Waterman captained Luke's team, while Third Alexander had chosen sides for his mates. Third now waved Rafe in from the outfield to take his place on the mound.

"I can't get it past the sonuvagun!" the towhead exclaimed in exasperation, handing the ball to the hard-throwing righty. The Barefoot Dodgers' weakness was in pitching. Only Buzz and Rafe could get it over the plate with any consistancy in games, when Third couldn't play. At seventeen, Third had led his high school team to the state championships last spring, and it sometimes galled him that his sibling could hit him at will. However, as his father had pointed out, Luke hit anything at will. He just couldn't run. The father figured that his younger son's ability came from an addiction to Atari games on the television screen, having read that the Air Force used the same system to teach hand-eye coordination to pilots.

Rafe's first pitch was a chest-high fastball, but not fast enough. The bat cracked, and Sherman Boatley chased the ball toward the corner, stopping in disgust as the sphere bounced into the stock pond, scattering the ducks and geese. "C'mon, Luke!" he yelled. "Keep it outa the pond!"

Junior Johnson called time from the infield while Sherman

shucked his jeans to wade out for the ball. "Aw right, guys," he instructed, "Let's do the CF Shift. Me and Jimmy Lee'll stay on each side of the infield, and the resta you get deep. Rafe, keep 'em high, so he'll hit flies."

Third and Sherman had retrieved the ball, and dried it off somewhat. Rafe's next offering was rifled straight back to him, for the first out, and the packed-outfield strategy worked, catching two of three, with the other centering a cow pie between Hey-Sue and Wilber Martin for a double. Third loped across the pasture for another baseball during the inning change; between the cattle and the pond, the one they had been using needed a rest, as Rafe noted. Buzz's team took the field.

First base was the only position Luke could play, since it required little running. All of the other players had learned over the years to watch for Luke's reddening face, or listen for his labored breathing, signs that he was in danger of heatstoke or a coughing spell. Only Hey-Sue and the Johnson boys, Junior and Blue Daddy, had little experience with Luke's illness, those families being new to Brownspur.

Hump Henderson stepped to the plate, swinging with his curious, yet powerful, short jerky stroke. Longmile's only son, Hump had been injured years before in a fall from a galloping mule during an outing with Third and Buzz. Either the actual fall or his youthful companions had moved Hump's broken shoulder in such a way that the small-town doctor was unable to correct. While the shoulder had healed, it was noticibly higher than the other, and did not allow full movement. Yet Hump was the best and most powerful hitter on the plantation, rivaling Luke in longball production. The difference, of course, was that Hump could run, though he did so with his head jutted forward and his short legs churning. Sort of like "an aggressive bowling ball with a bad attitude," as Third had once put it.

Third and Buzz often pitched together, and were too obviously the best pitchers on the plantation -- possibly the best overall athletes. They both wondered at the fact that the two most handicapped youngsters were the best hitters, and that one of them was a superb catcher.

The only other experienced catcher on the Barefoot Dodgers was Willy B Davidson, who didn't especially like the position, yet neither was he afraid to be behind the plate. In their pickup games during the past year, Hey-Sue had indicated an interest in learning to catch, but Hump refused to let him wear the catcher's gear. "Ain't no spic gonna put my stuff on," he declared to Willy B. "No tellin' what kinda cooties them folks got." By contrast, Hump had encouraged Luke to try playing behind the plate, since he wouldn't have to run much. However, Luke only had to try on Hump's equipment once to know he didn't want to be a catcher. The mask reminded him too much of the oxygen masks that were already such a hated part of his life, especially during his early years when CF had been diagnosed. He decided to take his chances at first, but it was hard not to run after a pop foul, or dive at a ball down the line. Once, when Luke had scared the hell out of Longmile with a bad coughing spell after chasing a foul into the catchpen fence, the coach had threatened to "nail yore foot to the base."

Longmile got the most out of his players, black, white, or brown. The Barefoot Dodgers had plenty of speed, with the likes of Willy B, Spider, Jimmy Lee Harris, and Rafe Jenkins. Many times these four bunted successfully for hits, and three pitches later would be on third, with stolen bases. The left-handed Jimmy Lee's specialty was to drag bunt, and Longmile was wont to call a sacrifice squeeze with a runner at third and Jimmy Lee at bat. One opposing team that the Dodgers played regularly, the Goose Hollow Giants, even had a special Jimmy Lee Shift, where the left fielder came in to play first, and the first sacker came in abreast of the pitcher's mound to take away the drag bunt.

Alternating the power of Hump and Caleb Spragins with the speedsters, interspersed with the consistent spray-hitting of Buzz and Sherman Boatley, gave the Dodgers quite an impressive offense. Wilber and Blue Daddy were the only weak hitters, and their teammates were inclined to blame that on the fact that these two were the only fathers on the team. Wilber was the oldest player, and least enthusiastic, married with two young children at home. Blue Daddy was barely eighteen, and had gotten a girl in trouble back in Georgia. He was a budding musician, but had left the promise of an Atlanta band for the safety of Mississippi, in the face of the wrath of an enraged father. "I got them weddin' bell blues" was the song Rafe teased him with. Rafe was also musically-inclined, and the two often jammed until late into the night at the plantation shop, where Mr. Leroy had agreed for them to practice, as long as there was no drinking. Rafe's daddy, Shorty Jenkins, was the plantation bee man, and had complained that his son's guitar accompanied by Blue Daddy's drums were simply too much for his bees. "They's off schedule on they honey-makin' and gettin' mean to boot!" he complained.

Defensively, the Dodgers' main weakness, as noted, was in their pitching. Buzz was the mound mainstay, with his roundhouse curves, change-ups, knuckleballs, and an occasional fastball mainly to keep the opposition off balance for his breaking stuff. He was tall and long-armed, in contrast to the shorter, hard-throwing Rafe, whose main problem was control. Both were right-handers, so Third was invaluable in practice to give the Dodgers a look at southpaw pitching. When Rafe was on, he was almost unbeatable, but Longmile never knew when he was going to be on or off. No one else could get it over the plate except Wilber, and his pitches had nothing on them.

The infield was adequate, with Spider -- who indeed looked like a spider, all arms and legs at shortstop -- being the star. Junior at third and Blue Daddy at second were passable, and when Buzz was playing first instead of pitching, his reach made their throws look great at times. When Buzz was on the mound, Jimmy Lee couldn't come up with errant throws. The outfield, with Rafe in center, flanked by Caleb and Willy B, was a ball-hawking trio. While Caleb was not as fast as the others, he had an uncanny knack for being in position to catch a ball. Longmile had long since given up trying to move Caleb to secondguess batters, and instead had made the boy the outfield captain, with the responsibility to position his mates.

In the practice games, with Third on first and Red Wood at third, the infield actually looked classy, for Blue Daddy tended to play up to the level of his fellow infielders. Red was flashy in the field, but weak at the plate, where his aggressiveness worked against him. He could clobber a fastball with regularity, but was a sucker for off-speed and breaking pitches. As with many redheads, he had a tendency to fly off the handle, and could be counted on to be the first into a brawl, coming off the fence when the Barefoot Dodgers were in a real game. Longmile had often told Red, "Son, I sho wish you was black!"

The only other regular on the Barefoot Dodgers was Buzz's younger brother, who was only twelve, and served as an outfield extra in practice or batboy during games. He was lighter of skin than Hey-Sue, and was called by even his own family, "Brown Brother."

Before Third had returned from his house with another ball, the evening bell bespoke chore time, and the game broke up, the players scattering to houses dotted about the 2000-acre plantation. "See ya tomorrow," floated in the Delta dusk.

TEAM **BareFooT Dodgers** RECORD TEAM RE

NO.	PLAYERS	B/A	POS INN	1	2	3	4	5	6
1	Willy B	RF							
	SUB. Brown Boo	RF	P4 6			i-3	F9		
	SUB.								
2	Jimmy Lee	1B							
	SUB. Sherman	2B 4				RBI			
	SUB.			E-3	6i				
3	Buzz	P 1B 4				F7		F7	
	SUB. III	1B 6							
	SUB.								
4	HUMP	C			F8			E6	
	SUB.				RBI			RBI	
	SUB.								
5	Caleb	LF		6-4			F8		
	SUB.								
	SUB.								
6	Spider	SS		6-4-3			6-3		
	SUB.					RBI			
	SUB.								
7	RAFE	CF P4			5-3	3-4			
	SUB. Hay-Sue	CF 4							
	SUB.								
8	Junior	3B		F9	4-3	K			
	SUB. Luke	PH 5							
	SUB. Red	3B PH 5							
9	Blue Paddy	2B		K					
	SUB. Wilbur	2B P 6			2 RBI				
	SUB.								
	SUB.								
	SUB.								
	Coach - Longmile								
	SUB.								
	SUB.								
UMPIRE Uncle Eb				4 3	3 2	1 1	1 0		
UMPIRE				LOB 1 / ER	LOB 3 / ER	LOB 1 / ER	LOB / ER	LOB / ER	LOB /
UMPIRE				E	E	E	E	E	E
SCORER				B/p		B/p			

Chapter Three

"Mr. Leroy, I need your advice," Longmile declared after tapping on the office door, which stood open. The plantation owner pushed his swivel chair away from the desk and stretched, glad of the interruption. He pulled the drink machine key from a drawer and pitched it to the stocky coach.

"Sure. Get us a couple of drinks."

He waved Longmile to a seat and both men propped their feet on the desk, the guest leaning back against the wall in a ladder-back chair. Each took a long swig, then Mr. Leroy slid a pint bottle of clear liquid from a file cabinet, and refilled his soft drink, passing the pint to Longmile as he shook up his bottle to blend the contents. "Sun's below the yardarm. Cheers, and thanks for breaking the routine grind."

Longmile shook his bottle and tasted gingerly. "Lordee! That Uncle Eb's stuff?"

"He claims he don't make it any more, but that a cousin gives it to him. Whatever, it's mighty smooth. I always make him take a swig when he brings me a bottle; then I put it up for a week to see if Uncle Eb's gonna die from it." They both grinned, and Mr. Leroy mock-toasted Longmile. "What's on your mind?"

"I got a call last week from a feller played with me at Shreveport, long time ago. He's front man for this league that's been up north for awhile, the International Amateur League, and they're wantin' to expand into the South. Found out I was one of the organizers of the state amateur league, and wanted to know would we be interested in joinin' up with the Internationals." He took a short pull at his drink and grimaced. "I never liked him much when we played together -- he was mean then -- but I got to admit he was a go-getter. Did a few years of major league ball with the Cards after I come back here. Says he's workin' for the league and coachin' a team himself in Mansfield."

He sipped again. "Anyway, you know we come durn close to the state title last year, and we're a year older and better now. These International Amateur League teams all swing down through here early in the spring -- you remember that Michigan team ole Rafe sold cuckleburrs to for a nickle apiece, tellin' 'em they was porcupine eggs? -- and we usually show up pretty good against them. They plan on havin' a national championship between the north and south in late August. I'd like to see how our boys would stand up to them big city ballplayers."

"What's it gonna cost?" the owner asked cynically.

Longmile grinned. "A hundred bucks to join the league, then another hundred for each tournament up to the nationals. We might get eliminated early and only be out a couple hundred. But if we won the state, and the southwide, that'd be four hundred at the outside."

"How about uniforms and equipment? We bought good tee shirts for jerseys last year, but most guys just play in jeans and sneakers. 'Course, I'm good for caps all around every spring. But nobody except Hump and Buzz has cleats. And you're gonna need travel money, if you win the state. You ain't gettin' into somethin' that's gonna cost an arm and a leg, are you?"

Longmile shrugged. "Ole John Henry mighta been playin' me for a sucker, but I don't think so. I've talked to several of the other coaches, and it seems like you can go as high class as you want. Shoot, if we start winnin' we'll make the team earn their own money. Surely they can do somethin' to keep playin' baseball until cotton pickin' time."

Mr. Leroy fingered an envelope on the edge of his desk. "Tell you what," he mused, "I just got this in last week. Bubba Duncan's Cotton Company is offering a premium for the first bale of cotton in the Delta this year that'll amount to nearly two thousand dollars. If these guys want to get out and make a run for it when that early field starts opening up in the deadening, I'll donate the whole thing to the Barefoot Dodgers -- win, lose, or draw!"

Longmile nearly choked on his drink, and flopped his feet off the desk as his chair legs hit the floor. "Two thousand bucks! Them boys'll play the Yankees for that!"

"They'd have to pick the first bale to make the money, but that's my deal. If they're earliest with the cotton, we'll use the prize money on the team -- uniforms, bases, equipment, shoes, travel -- whatever you decide, Coach." The planter stuck out his hand. "Deal?"

Longmile shook on it: "Deal!"

A hand-filled baseball scorecard for the team "Barefoot Dodgers."

NO.	PLAYERS	B/A	POS/INN	1	2	3	4	5	6
1	Willy B / SUB. Brown Boo / SUB.	RF / RF	PH/6			1-3	F9		
2	Jimmy Lee / SUB. Sherman / SUB.	1B / 2B	4	E3	L7	RBI			
3	Buzz / SUB. III / SUB.	P / 1B	1B/4 /6			F9		F7	
4	Hump / SUB. / SUB.	C		F8 / RBI			E4 / RBI		
5	Caleb / SUB. / SUB.	LF		6-4			F8		
6	Spider / SUB. / SUB.	SS		6-4-3	1-0	6-3 / RBI			
7	Rafe / SUB. Hay-Sue / SUB.	CF / CF	P/4 /4		5-3	3-4			
8	Junior / SUB. Luke / SUB. Red	3B / / 3B	PH/5 PH/5	F9	4-3	K			
9	Blue Daddy / SUB. Wilbur 6th / SUB.	2B / 2B	P/6		K	2 RBI			
	SUB. / SUB.								
	Coach - Longmile / SUB. / SUB.								
UMPIRE	Uncle Eb		R 4 3 / LOB 1 / ER	R 3 2 H / LOB 1 / ER	R 1 H / LOB 1 / OER	R 1 0 H / LOB 1 / ER	R / LOB / ER	R / LOB
UMPIRE				E	E	E	E	E	E
UMPIRE									
SCORER				B/P	B/P				

TEAM: Barefoot Dodgers   RECORD   TEAM   RE

Chapter Four

"It looked extremely rocky for the Mudville Nine that day..." Luke quoted as he marked another K in the scorebook.

Longmile grunted. "What's that?"

The CF Kid shook his head as Uncle Eb called the first pitch to Caleb a strike. "First line from a poem called 'Casey at the Bat.' Looks pretty bad for us right now. This Goose Hollow guy is throwin' asprin tablets!"

Buzz nodded agreement. "Lest you change that scratch bunt Spider beat out from an error, we ain't gonna get a hit off this dude. Bad thing is, I ain't pitched po'ly myself!"

Luke shook his head again. "If the third baseman hadn't bobbled it, Spider never woulda beat it out. And if Willy B hadn't slipped on that cow pie, he'da caught that triple that cleared the bases. We'd only be down two runs instead of five. 'Course," he added judiciously, "Willy B didn't walk two batters that inning, either."

Buzz scowled. "Uncle Eb just wouldn't gimme that corner, is all. Hump never moved his mitt." The Barefoot Dodger captain rose and grabbed his glove as the umpire in question called a third strike on his own son for the last out. "Okay, Dodgers, let's go after 'em. Only two more innings!" The lanky pitcher loped toward the mound.

On the fence behind the bench, Third Alexander leaned to whisper to Red Wood. "Reckon there's only one thing to do?" His companion nodded agreement and reached into his pocket for a coin. "Heads," Third called the flip. Heads it was, and the towhead sighed, swiveled, dropped into the catch pen, and disappeared around the corner of the commissary. Less than ten minutes later, he was climbing back onto the fence. "I miss anything?" he asked.

"Nah. First batter fouled off seven pitches and Longmile had to call time to find a ball. Buzz finally walked him and they put on the hit-and-run, but Blue Daddy was lookin' for it and doubled 'em up. Witch Doctor didn't see you?"

"They were out in the garden pickin' okra. I got clean away. They oughta be here any second." Third pointed toward the right field corner. "Here they come now!" he exclaimed, just as the Goose Hollow catcher popped to Junior for the third out.

The Witch Doctor was a Brownspur tenant who purportedly had magical powers. Third had once heard his father opine, "It ain't that he can actually DO magic; it's just that he's got everybody BELIEVIN' that he can do magic." The elderly man and his wife kept pretty much to themselves, but tales circulated in even faraway communities of his talents, and often there were cars parked at his house with tags from exotic places like California, New York, and Illinois. Love potions, healing medicines, and special spells were reportedly bought by people from all over, and one jealous wife had even purchased a "gris-gris" which had killed her husband. Even Mr. Leroy believed that the man had died because of the spell, though he pointed out to his boys that, "The spell didn't kill Vernell; he just gave himself up to die when he heard there was a gris-gris on him. Hell, I even offered to pay for liftin' it, but he had just given up."

The Witch Doctor's home was just across the old "Black Dog" dummy line from the commissary and pasture where the Dodgers played ball. In past years the Bogue & Delta Line railroad tracks had been taken up, and the line abandoned, but residents whose communities had once been serviced by the B&D, or Black Dog Line, still referred to themselves as "livin' on the Dog." The Bogue & Delta Line was paralleled thirty miles to the east by the still-existant Yazoo & Delta Line, which was called the "Yellow Dog" by its communities.

The Barefoot Dodgers had come to believe over the past couple of years that whenever the Witch Doctor's hogs escaped from the pen and wandered onto the field (they were invariably attracted to the grain stored in the haybarn by right field) that the team fortunes would change for the better. On days when a Dodger could not buy a hit, the appearance of the "Rally Pigs," as they became known, would change the aforementioned aspirin tablets to gopher balls. Insuring the escape of the hogs had been the mission Third and Red had flipped for.

"Rally Pigs!" Willy B hissed as he threw his glove under the bench and reached for a bat. "They're out in right!"

Hump jerked around to see as he unbuckled his shin guards. "Aw right! Now we got this guy's number! Watch me park the first pitch." He grinned as he swaggered toward the box, causing the Giant catcher to frown suspiciously. Uncle Eb, behind the plate, smiled into his mask. The Barefoot Dodger bench, dead quiet before, began to chant, "HUMP, HUMP, HUMP, HUMP," in time with that worthy's strides as he neared the batter's box. Luke was the first to turn his cap around, passing the scorebook to Buzz to show HR already marked for Hump's turn at bat. The CF Kid swung to look at his brother, who winked and motioned thumbs up.

The Giant coach stood and stepped forward to see what the sudden commotion was about. "Time, Mr. Ump," he called. "Lemme run them pigs away from right field." Uncle Eb stopped the game while the outfielders chased the grunting hogs past the foul line, then motioned "Play ball" as soon as the centerfielder was back in position. The first pitch to the supremely confident Hump, sure enough, was blasted over the fielder's head, past the stock pond, and rolled into the mockorange hedge around the Alexander's back yard. The Barefoot Dodgers batted around against the Giant starter and two relievers, and Buzz retired the visitors in the ninth on five knuckleballs, to win by a run. The Goose Hollow Giants never knew what had hit them: the Rally Pigs.

"Aw right, you guys," yelled Longmile. "Mr. Leroy's got cold drinks in the store -- but y'all run out there and get them hogs back in the pen before you come in." The coach turned to Third and Red, grinning. "And you two fencesitters go help 'em!"

Mr. Leroy leaned on one knee, propped up on the porch bench. He chuckled, "Way to go, Coach! You sure know how to rally your team, doncha?"

Uncle Eb answered him from just behind Longmile. "As a man believeth in his heart, so can he hit a baseball," he paraphrased a Bible quote. "Who let them hogs out, Longmile? I oughta throw that player outa the next game," the umpire teased.

"White boys let them hogs out, and I didn't have nothin' to do with it," the coach declared stoutly. "But, Mr. Leroy, you really oughta send a sack of corn over 'cross the tracks. The Witch Doctor's awful accomodatin' 'bout them hogs gettin' out when there's a baseball game."

The plantation owner nodded agreement. "You take it, okay? All the boys are scared of 'im. They just go over there when y'all get behind. I knew where Third was headed when I saw him zip by the window. What you gonna do if you win the state, Longmile? Carry those hogs to St. Louis with you?"

"If I had alla your money, and was really pullin' for the Barefoot Dodgers, I'd buy one of them shoats and barbeque it and send it with the team, sho'nuff." He winked at Uncle Eb.

"Caught in my own web," Mr. Leroy laughed. "Longmile, you win the state, and we'll sure eat a barbequed Rally Pig!"

"Y'all better not tell 'em before then," Uncle Eb advised. "Ain't nothin' to them pigs, but them boys do believe in 'em. They found out you was gonna kill and eat one, they'd lose just as sure as the world."

Mr. Leroy moved to unlock the drink machine as the team began trooping into the store, laughing at Rafe and Red, who had both fallen headlong in the mud heading off a shoat. Longmile softly asked Uncle Eb, "You don't really believe that Witch Doctor put some kinda lucky spell on them hogs, do you?"

The older man gently rebuked the coach. "Bible says not to mess with black magic and junk like that." He paused, then spoke again. "But I wouldn't tell them boys there ain't nothin' to it until after the season, if I was you! That Giant pitcher was throwin' just as good as before, but our boys all of a sudden just knew they could hit 'im. Hump hit a fastball that I bet was close to a hunnerd miles an hour!" Uncle Eb shook his head. "I'll teach 'em Sunday School; you just coach 'em, Longmile. If it takes Rally Pigs to win, well...."

"Root Beer, Uncle Eb?" Third Alexander offered a drink to the umpire. "That was some last inning, huh?"

"Sure was, chile. Thanks." The old man winked.

TEAM *Barefoot Dodgers*   RECORD ____ TEAM ____ RE___

NO.	PLAYERS	B/A	POS/INN	1	2	3	4	5	6
1	Willy B	RF				1-3	F9		
	SUB. Brown Bro	RF	PH/6						
2	Jimmy Lee	1B							
	SUB. Sherman	2B	/4	E3	61	RBI			
3	Buzz	P	1B/4			F7		F7	
	SUB. III	1B	/6						
	SUB.								
4	Hump	C			F8			E4	
	SUB.				RBI			RBI	
	SUB.								
5	Caleb	LF		6-4			F8		
	SUB.								
	SUB.								
6	Spider	SS		6-4-3	1		6-3		
	SUB.						RBI		
	SUB.								
7	Rafe	CF	P/4		5-3	3-4			
	SUB. Hay-Sue	CF	/4						
	SUB.								
8	Junior	3B		F9	4-3	K			
	SUB. Luke		PH/5						
	SUB. Red	3B	PH/5						
9	Blue Daddy	2B			K				
	SUB. Wilbur 6th	2B	P/6			2 RBI			
	SUB.								
	SUB.								
	SUB.								
	Coach - Longmile								
	SUB.								
	SUB.								
UMPIRE *Uncle Eb*				R4 3	R3 2 H	R1 1 H	R1 0 H	R	R
UMPIRE				LOB1 1 ER	LOB2 1 ER	LOB1 0 ER	LOB1 1 ER	LOB ER	LOB
UMPIRE				E	E	E	E	E	E
SCORER				B/P		B/P			

Chapter Five

The game against the Isola Eagles had been rained out, not a usual situation for the Brownspur summers. The Barefoot Dodgers had retreated to the dusky confines of the haybarn after Mr. Leroy had made the telephone call to inform the Eagles' coach that the field was far too wet and it was still raining. Rafe was strumming absently on his guitar while Junior cut a piece of grapevine into finger-length sections. Caleb warned in his slow drawl, "Y'all ought not be smokin' up here 'round all this hay."

Red scoffed, "We do it all the time. You just gotta be careful. Gimme one, Junior."

Several of the boys chewed tobacco, but few of them smoked it yet. Marijuana had not yet reached into the rural South from its widespread use in the north and far west, though southern city youths had embraced it for some years, for Junior and Blue Daddy recalled its pungency from the times when they lived near Atlanta. Farm boys often began experimenting with smoking on grapevine or a wild herb called "rabbit tobacco" -- more properly Fragrant Cudweed -- which was dried briefly, rolled into cigarette papers and puffed while somewhat green. Neither was particularly addictive nor harmful, as far as anyone knew. Nor was it very good to smoke; it was simply a rite of passage.

Brown Brother glanced sideways at Buzz and extended his hand for a length of grapevine. When his older brother didn't veto it, he leaned forward to puff it into life from Red's already lit piece. Luke shook his head at the offer from Third, knowing he could not afford to inflict his lungs with anything. By the time Brown Brother took his first real drag of grapevine smoke, most of the other boys were puffing away. No one was prepared for the youngster's reaction.

"A-Huck, A-huck!" Brown Brother coughed. Suddenly, his eyes bugged out and he retched violently, the piece of grapevine slipping unnoticed from his fingers as Buzz reached a long arm to whack him on the back. Luke pulled a handkerchief from his pocket to wipe the boy's mouth while Willy B held his head up. Caleb was the first to see the smoke.

"Hey! He's done set the damn barn on fire!" It was one of the few times they could remember Caleb losing his composure, but there was little time to comment on it. Flames leaped from the hay bale Brown Brother had been sitting on. "Fire!" yelled Caleb again, as several voices joined in.

The haybarn was a huge cypress wood structure nearly fifty years old. It was probably seventy-five feet long, forty feet wide, and thirty feet high. And it was filled about two-thirds full of dry oat straw and alfalfa hay bales. "OhmyGod!" Third exclaimed. "If Daddy finds out..."

Buzz grabbed his sibling and vaulted from the stack. "Out!" he bellowed. "Get out of here, you and Luke. Get those fire extinguishers outa the shop! Get some help! Run!" he ordered.

It was Spider whose instincts saved the barn. Grabbing the flaming bale by the wire strands that held it wrapped tightly, he slung the burning bundle down into the clear center aisle. "Never mind gettin' water!" he yelled. "Get the burnin' bales outta the barn, quick!" He slung a second after the first as Red grabbed another to follow suit. Acrid smoke stung the Dodgers' eyes as bale after bale caught fire and was thrown down. Below in the aisle, Buzz, Hump, Jimmy Lee, and Blue Daddy shoved the burning bales outside into the rain, while stomping at flames that threatened other stacks. Brown Brother and Luke had run for the nearby plantation shop, where Red's father kept several fire extinguishers. The CF Kid could not keep pace, though, and had a severe coughing spell, spitting phlegm and choking, unable to tell his companion by his motions to keep on toward the shop and to spread the alarm. Brown Brother turned back and sprinted to the barn, panicked.

"Luke's dyin'!" he screamed to Buzz, ducking the fiery bale his big brother was tossing into the barnyard.

With all the commotion inside, Buzz was the only one to hear this terrifying new pronouncement. Grabbing the one who had precipitated all the action, the Dodger captain sprinted out into the rain, unaware that he was holding his little brother completely off the wet ground by the scruff of the neck and shirt collar. In seconds, he was kneeling at the coughing, red-faced figure, who was still unable to speak. Scooping Luke up in his arms, Buzz ran for the shelter of the shop, which was unoccupied. Brown Brother hurried to open the door. An oxygen-acetylene torch rig stood next to the electric welder, and Luke pointed feebly to it, still coughing. Buzz dumped the contents of Mr. Wood's huge toolbox onto the cement floor, looking for a screwdriver.

Grasping the tool, he quickly loosened the wormgear clamp on the oxygen hose, jerked the hose end from its fitting on the cutting torch, and handed the end to Luke as he opened the valve on the oxygen tank, first checking to be sure that the acetylene valve was closed. Brown Brother's terror -- for he was blaming himself for both burning the barn and killing Luke -- subsided visibly as Luke began to breathe, still spitting phlegm. Buzz hugged his trembling sibling in relief.

Luke's left hand jerked out almost convulsion-like as he held the hose to his face with his right. "He's havin' a fit!" exclaimed Brown Brother, but Luke's wide eyes were completely sane. Shaking his head, he again thrust his arm toward the wall. Buzz misunderstood the gesture, which was in the direction of town, seven miles away.

"You want us to get you to a hospital?"

The answer was a fierce scowl and a jerk of the hose away from the mouth as the CF Kid choked out, "The fire, dammit!"

"Sonuva...I forgot!" Buzz jumped for the extinguisher on the shop wall that Luke was indicating. Grabbing a second from behind the parts room door, he instructed Brown Brother forcibly, "Stay here with Luke and keep him quiet!" and sprinted back into the rain.

Smoldering hay bales dotted the barnyard, but there was no longer a column of smoke hovering above the barn. Most of the smoke was trapped in the barn still, and the Dodger captain could hear the cries of his comrades and the thump of bales hitting the floor of the aisle. Willy B staggered out as Buzz raced up. The wiry right fielder's eyes were pouring tears, and he was coughing almost as bad as Luke had been. "Is it out?" Buzz gasped.

Willy B obviously did not recognize his friend. "Yeah, man, we done got the fire bales outside, but we done lost a guy. We scared he fell down and smotherated under some of that hay in all that smoke. Help us!"

"Oh, God, please...." Buzz mumbled as he started into the smoky interior, just in time to be bowled over by a hacking, choking Hump, his eyes also gushing. But the catcher could still see, barely. "Buzz! That you? You okay? Where the hell.... Hey, guys, Buzz is out here!"

"Y'all lookin' for me?"

"Hell, yes!" Red Wood stormed out. "We done thrown down another ten tons of hay what wasn't burnt, thinkin' you was under some of it! Who's gonna stack all that hay back up? Not me! Dadgummit, Buzz, you oughta let us know when you run off...." He broke off, coughing and retching.

Jimmy Lee and Junior, supporting Third between them, appeared from the smoke. "Everybody out!" bellowed Caleb, right behind them, and pushing for a breath of fresh air. "Head count! Dad blame it, Buzz! How come you run off? We been lookin' for you in all that smoke under all that hay...." An enraged roar interrupted his tirade. Blue Daddy emerged from the barn's dimness, dragging a struggling Rafe.

"My guitar! Sherman stepped smack dab in the middle of my guitar! I'm gonna kill 'im...." Rafe ranted between coughs.

Sherman and Spider were the last two Dodgers out of the smoking barn, the latter falling to his back in the barnyard and opening his mouth to the cooling raindrops. "Where you been while we was fightin' fire, Buzz?" he queried weakly. "You gotta stack all that hay back by yourownself. I don't never wanta see another bale of hay or a grapevine!"

"Hey, you guys," the object of their concern declared, "I sent Brown Brother and Luke after these fire extinguishers and Luke had a coughin' fit and I hadta go after 'em and rescue Luke and get him to the shop for some oxygen and...."

"He okay?" Hump asked, still lying just outside the barn door, head propped up on one hand wearily.

"Think so," was the reply. "I'm headed back to check, since y'all got the fire out. You are sure it's out, ain'tcha? I'll leave these extinguishers for y'all just in case."

The captain turned to lope away, then stopped after three strides to face his exhausted mates again. Third and Jimmy Lee were bent over the same bale, vomiting from smoke inhalation. Hump, Spider, and Sherman still lay prone. The rest slumped wearily on wet bales of hay, some of which smoldered despite the slackening rain. Rafe wept over his smashed guitar, which had cost him more than forty dollars. Buzz directed his question to Junior Johnson.

"Hey, Junior, you got some more grapevine? I need a smoke!"

He managed to get his back turned and took the fairly fresh cow pie on his shoulder, though much of the manure splattered satisfactorily across his neck. The Dodger captain raced away laughing as his catcher exclaimed admiringly, "Willy B, you oughta try pitchin', could you chunk a baseball as good as you do a fresh cow pie!"

Chapter Six

An area tournament was scheduled for the following weekend at nearby Trilakes Plantation, whose owner had fallowed the field next to the Growling Cubs regular diamond. With some tractor work, a second diamond had been laid out back-to-back with the original field, and Mr. Leroy had sent the Barefoot Dodgers' bases and plate down so that two games could be played simultaneously. As an added attraction, the two plantation owners agreed to split the cost of a fish fry that Saturday night. The Trilakes regular field was one of the few lighted diamonds in the area, and the championship game was to be played after dark. Teams from Goose Hollow, DunDeal, and Daylight Plantations, as well as town teams from Isola, Rolling Fork and Morgan City, joined the fray.

Mr. Leroy's joint venture in the fish fry had committed him to provide the fish for frying. On Wednesday, he met with the Barefoot Dodgers at practice. "Boys, that's a lot of mouths to feed. We're gonna hafta seine the creek."

Longmile interpreted: "When Mr. Leroy says 'we gotta seine,' he ain't talkin' about him and me and Uncle Eb. We too old to get down in there with them water moccasins any more. That means you all gotta seine the creek. Meet me here early tomorrow. Buzz, you and Spider and Willy B hustle up some chinaberry poles, thick as your wrist and about six feet long -- 'bout a dozen. Red, get your daddy to let us have that old chicken-wire fence he tore down last fall and left rolled up. You and Third have it here in the mawnin'. Rest of you, bring wash tubs, ice chests, knives and spoons for scalin'. What else, Mr. Leroy?"

"I'll run into town early and get some block ice. Wear boots or ruint sneakers to wade in. Uncle Eb, can you have some snakebite medicine available, just in case?"

The old man shrugged. "I think my cousin still makes some of that stuff. I'll borry some."

The morning dawned clear on a team engaged with wire cutters, hammers, staples, and chinaberry poles. The old chicken wire fence was cut into sections four feet high and twelve feet long, to each end of which were secured poles. These seines were loaded into Red's father's and Mr. Leroy's pickups, along with the washtubs, ice chests, boys, and snakebite medicine. Along the winding creek which meandered through Brownspur, the fishermen took turns. While Luke and Mr. Leroy stood snakeguard with .22 rifles on the banks, the boys would grasp the poles at each end and stretch the wire across the creek. Two pairs would start about a hundred yards apart and wade toward each other, splashing and sloshing as they dragged the seine forward. As the gap closed, the panicked fish -- and snakes, turtles, frogs, crawfish, lamp eels, or other trapped aquatic life -- would begin to surface and thrash in the muddied water between the seines.

When the distance between had narrowed to perhaps thirty yards, another seine would be started, dragging crossways the creek, where the fish were most concentrated. The trapped denizens would be quickly dumped onto the bank to be sorted by the boys: snakes were dispatched forthwith, fish were flipped into the waiting tubs, bullfrogs were bashed with sticks and stuffed into a gunny sack, crawfish were scooped into a separate large ice chest for purging and boiling. Uncle Eb relished eels, and Rafe claimed the stray furbearer harvested -- muskrat, nutria, or once a full-grown beaver -- for his father, who trapped and sold hides, besides keeping bees for some of the plantation's "long sweetning," as honey and molasses were called.

No fish were culled except the occasional bony shad. Bass,

bream, catfish, carp, buffalo, gaspar ghoul, and gar went into the pot after cleaning. Mr. Wood had drafted a dozen team mothers and fathers for fish cleaning duty at the shop, and as each stretch of creek yielded its booty, a pickup truck would make a run back to the cleaning station to deliver fish. Buzz's mother had two pots heating for the anticipated crawfish harvest, and had Brown Brother standing by to "purge" the mudbugs, by immersing them in salty water so that the creatures expelled the mud in their systems before they were boiled.

The Dodgers had excitement aplenty. Once a big stumptail moccasin charged Caleb, and Luke's excited volley, while it did kill the snake, nearly hit Willy B. Another enraged moccasin ambushed Junior from where it had crawled onto the bank, and only a warning scream from Red had enabled Junior to dodge the strike. A third cottonmouth had been seined onto the bank unnoticed until the sorting began, and Sherman had actually picked the serpent up before slinging it in a panic toward Longmile, who bowled over Spider and Hump trying to escape. "I thought it was a catfish," Sherman claimed lamely. Spider's ankle was slightly sprained, and Mr. Leroy iced it down before relegating the shortstop to truck-driving duty for the rest of the day.

A huge alligator gar, nearly six feet long, was trapped momentarily by the advancing seines, and finally decided to escape through the wire. Blue Daddy and Third, holding those particular poles, were jerked backward and sideways into the water, and the wire ripped completely away from the poles. No one had ever seen a gar that big in the creek, and Mr. Leroy's yell of "Alligator gar" was understood to be "Alligator!" That cleared the creek of all within earshot, including Wilber and Jimmy Lee, pulling the other approaching seine. That drag was a total waste, and the next section of creek was skipped, that being the direction the gar had departed.

Two seines later, the beaver was trapped, and made an attempt to escape just as the gar had done, through the wire. Buzz and Hump were pulling the seine, and assumed by the weight and power of the unseen creature that they had again encountered the huge gar. Knowing that the jaws of a gar that size could crush their submerged legs, they abandoned their seine to scramble up the bank to safety, but the beaver had become entangled in the wire. While the seine was wrecked, they did dispatch the beaver for Shorty Jenkins.

Weary, muddy, wet, and happy, the Barefoot Dodgers finally ceased their efforts after noon, and returned to the shop, where Mr. Leroy proclaimed that more than enough fish had been caught for the weekend tournament fry. The boys washed up at the nurse tank station, the two-inch hydrant where the farm tractor spray tanks were filled, and reentered the shop where wide boards had been placed atop sawhorses to form a long table, upon which had been dumped boiled crawfish and the vegetables cooked in the same pot: corn, potatoes, and onions fresh from the garden. Mr. Leroy pitched the drink machine key to Third, who recruited Hey-Sue and Brown Brother to trot over to the commissary with him and bring back two cases of cold drinks. As an afterthought, the towhead snagged three loaves of light bread for the table. Adults and youngsters dug into the feast, though Blue Daddy and Junior were reluctant to try the crawfish. Buzz shrugged at their squeamishness: "That's okay; just more for the rest of us."

Shorty showed up with two gallons of honeycomb to put the finishing touches on the feast. As the adults and Barefoot Dodgers chewed the sweet wax, Willy B commented, "Guys, if we don't win that tournament this weekend, it ain't gonna be 'cause we're starvin' to death. Spider, how's the ankle?"

"I'll play," the shortstop declared. "Somebody just warn me

when Coach runs my direction, next time!"

Mr. Leroy stuck his head in the door. "Clean up time, boys. Third, y'all load all the fish guts, heads, and leavin's into my pickup."

"Aw, Daddy..." his son started to protest, but the father stopped him with a raised hand.

"Y'all ain't gotta take 'em far. I asked the Witch Doctor if he'd like the leftovers for his hogs. Just take the stuff across the Dog. Longmile's goin' with you."

"Aw right!" Luke exclaimed. "We make the Rally Pigs happy too, we'll sure take that tournament!"

"Yeah!" his father agreed. "Longmile, stop by the commissary on your way back. Uncle Eb says he's got some of that snakebite medicine left over, and you know that stuff won't keep." The plantation owner held out his hand to his oldest son, who dug in his pocket and returned the drink machine key.

Hump and Wilber swung a garbage can full of fish cleanings into the bed of the pickup. "Rally Pigs gonna be happy tonight!" the catcher declared.

NO.	PLAYERS	B/A	POS/INN	1	2	3	4	5	6
1	Willy B	RF				1-3	F9		
	SUB. Brown Bro	RF	PH/6						
2	Jimmy Lee	1B							
	SUB. Sherman	2B	/4	E3	61	RBI			
3	Buzz	P	1B/4			F7		F7	
	SUB. III	1B	/6						
4	Hump	C			F8			E6	
	SUB.				RBI			RBI	
	SUB.								
5	Caleb	LF		6-4				F8	
	SUB.								
	SUB.								
6	Spider	SS		6-4-3			6-3		
	SUB.						RBI		
	SUB.								
7	Rafe	CF	P/4		5-3	3-4			
	SUB. Hay-Sue	CF	/4						
	SUB.								
8	Junior	3B		F9	4-3	K			
	SUB. Luke		BB/5						
	SUB. Red	3B	PH/5						
9	Blue Daddy	2B			K				
	SUB. Wilbur 4th	2B	P/6			2 RBI			
	SUB.								
	SUB.								
	Coach - Longmile								
	SUB.								
	SUB.								
UMPIRE	Uncle Eb			R 4 3 LOB1 ER	R 3 2 H LOB2 ER 1	R 1 H LOB1 ER	R 0 H LOB1 ER	R LOB ER	R LOB
UMPIRE				E	E	E	E	E	E
UMPIRE									
SCORER				B/B	B/B				

The Barefoot Dodgers

Chapter Seven

Though Trilakes Plantation was less than ten miles from Brownspur, it had missed the rain which had helped extinguish the haybarn fire, and was in the midst of a month-long drought. The fallow field upon which an extra baseball diamond had been laid out had been deep-broken, chisel plowed, disked several times, and harrowed well in the weeks before the scheduled tournament. Everyone had expected some rain to settle the earth, but that had not come about. The extra diamond was just dust -- about six inches deep.

Coaches from the tournament teams walked across the field that Saturday morning, their footprints inches deep in the soft soil. "We can't play baseball on this!" Huey Morrison of the Rolling Fork Rooters declared, kicking disgustedly and then dodging as the dust blew right back in his face.

"We already got it lined off, and the bases and plate down," growled Pot Simmons, the host coach. "I say let's try it. Both teams will be playin' on it, so it ain't gonna hurt anybody worse than the other. Only alternative would be to have two teams playin' on our regular diamond, and sendin' two teams to play at another field somewhere, like Brownspur or Goose Hollow, and that'd ruin the schedulin'."

Longmile shrugged. "Our bases and plate are down here. We'd have to pull 'em up and take 'em back and put 'em back down. What can it hurt to try?" The other coaches nodded agreement.

"Shoot, we already over here now," Jimbo Gines noted. "And I ain't goin' back to Morgan City 'fore that fish fry tonight!"

"Okay," Pot declared, "here're the rules: seven innin' games, except for the championship one tonight; single elimination. We gotta home run derby that'll be open to all teams as well as the spectators durin' the fish fry 'fore the final game. Figgerin' two hours per game, with the first startin' at nine, playin' on both diamonds, okay? Let's go play ball!"

Longmile realized during the warmups that they had made a mistake. "Sonuvagun!" he exclaimed to Decker Watkins, coach of the Goose Hollow Giants. "The ball ain't gonna bounce! It's just gonna bury up in that dust. We can't play baseball in this stuff, Decker."

Simmons was not convinced, however, and as host, his team would be playing on the good diamond for the opening game. "We done decided, guys. Let's at least try it."

The Giants and Barefoot Dodgers opened play on the extra diamond, Buzz pitching. He immediately protested: "Coach, there ain't nothin' but a pile of knee-high dust out there for a mound! What I'm gonna stand on to pitch?"

"Your foots, far as I know, Buzz. Try it and see what happens. We're down here now. Their pitcher ain't gonna have a mound, either."

It was a farce.

Every pitch hit into the ground simply stopped within a foot or so of its initial contact with the deep dust. On long fly balls, unless they were hit almost directly to someone, the outfielders were unable to make running plays. "It's like runnin' in sand!" Willy B exclaimed. "Shoot, it's worse'n that! Quicksand!"

On the other hand, baserunners having to slog through the loamy soil took nearly twice as long to get to a base. It was quickly clear that there would be no basestealing on the extra diamond. The leadoff Giant batter topped one of Buzz's changeups, which stopped not halfway to Blue Daddy. On the first pitch to the next hitter, the leadoff took off to steal second. Hump's peg was on the money, and the normally speedy runner was scarcely more than halfway. He tried to go back, but was easily caught in a rundown. "We can't play in this stuff!" he spat disgustedly on his way back to the dugout.

That was the only out for awhile, however. Buzz was pitching his normal consistant game, and the Giant hitters as usual were topping his offerings, so that on a regular field, Blue and Spider would have assisted for three outs in the first seven pitches. Yet in the deep dust, balls stopped almost where they first hit the ground. Hump and Buzz found themselves having to charge almost as if for bunts, except charging was impossible. Longmile called time after two runs had scored and the bases were loaded with one out, all on balls to the infield -- and no one had errored! The coach called even his outfielders to the mound.

"This is crazy, but we can't call it now. Buzz, you throwin' good; can you keep it up?"

His captain was frustrated. "What I'm gonna do, Longmile? This is a joke! They ain't even hit once to the outfield and have almost batted around."

"Calm down. Can you keep the ball down?"

"He's okay," Hump answered. "But he and I can't keep this up. We need a strikeout pitcher on this field, but even if we bring Rafe in, he ain't got no mound to work from."

"Okay, here's what we'll try. They ain't hit a ball further than the pitcher. Junior, you play halfway down the line, and Blue, you do the same on the first base side. We gotta force at the plate now. Outfielders, play in so you're almost at deep infield, except Rafe -- you're the only regular-depth outfielder. Buzz, make 'em either hit it in the dirt or pop up, okay?"

Decker Watkins nodded in agreement as the Dodgers shifted around. He had already decided to switch to his own junkballer, and to employ a similar strategy if and when the Giants took the field. "Try to poke it over the infield," he advised his hitter.

Who tried, and popped up to Willy B just behind second. The next batter chopped one into the dust at Blue Daddy's feet, closer to home plate than Buzz on the so-called pitcher's mound. Blue fired to the plate for the force, and Hump still had plenty of time to throw to first to beat the slogging runner.

It went like that for both teams. Even playing seven innings, it still took nearly three hours to finish the game, and the final score was 28-26, the Giants winning. Buzz, Rafe, and Wilber had all three pitched for the Dodgers, and the Giants had ended up using four hurlers themselves. Luke used four score sheets to record 46 hits for the Giants, and 41 for the Dodgers. Spider and Willy B had both gone 8 for 9 with 6 runs. "Buzz, your ERA is about 76.32, near as I can figure," the CF Kid announced. "That's gotta be a record!"

"Lemme tell you where to stick your record," Buzz declared in disgust.

The two games on the Dust Diamond, as they called it, lasted a combined seven hours and fifteen minutes, the Rooters beating the Mockingbirds 34-27 in the second game, with a total of 94 hits and 17 errors. Two of the Morgan City players collapsed with heat exhaustion, and Jimbo Gines had to borrow Third to pitch the final inning for his team. The scheduled third game on the Dust Diamond was shifted to the regular Trilakes field, since the third game of that bracket had been a fast-moving pitcher's duel, won by the Growlers 1-0.

The Growlers then easily beat the exhausted Rooters for the tourney championship, having never had to play on the extra field. The Barefoot Dodgers got one measure of revenge, however, for Hump and Luke finished first and second in the Home Run Derby, winning the prizes of fifty and twenty-five bucks, respectively. At Sherman's suggestion, they pooled their money to buy Rafe a new guitar, with the left-over cash going into a fund for the state championship expenses.

"I heard they was gonna play the state tournament on the Trilakes baseball complex," Red Wood noted innocently, as he helped Buzz and Wilber collect the Brownspur bases after the fish fry.

"And call it the Dust Bowl!" the Dodger captain snorted, throwing first base at the redhead.

TEAM **Barefoot Dodgers** RECORD _____ TEAM _____ RE...

NO.	PLAYERS	B/A	POS INN	1	2	3	4	5	6
1	Willy B	RF				1-3	F9		
	SUB. Brown Bro	RF	P4						
2	Jimmy Lee	1B							
	SUB. Sherman	2B	4	E3	L7	RBL			
3	Buzz	P	1B 4			F7		F7	
	SUB. III	1B	6						
4	Hump	C			F8			E6	
	SUB.				RBL			RBL	
5	Caleb	LF		6-4				F8	
	SUB.								
6	Spider	SS		1-4-3	1-0		C-3		
	SUB.						RBL		
7	Rafe	CF P4			5-3		3-4		
	SUB. Hay-Sue	CF	4						
8	Junior	3B		F9		4-3	K		
	SUB. Luke		P4 S						
	SUB. Red	3B	P4 S						
9	Blue Daddy	2B			K				
	SUB. Wilbur	4th 2B	P6				2 RBL		
	SUB.								
	SUB.								
	Coach - Longmile								
	SUB.								
	SUB.								
UMPIRE	Uncle Eb			R 4 3	R 3 2	R 1 1	R 1 0	R	R
UMPIRE				LOB 1 ER	LOB 2 ER	LOB 1 ER	LOB 1 ER	LOB ER	LOB
UMPIRE				E	E	E	E	E	E
SCORER				Bp		Bp			

Chapter Eight

The hot, dry weather that summer caused the early cotton in the deadening field to begin opening earlier than expected. One morning Longmile hailed his employer before he could leave the barns after instructing the tractor drivers concerning the day's activities.

"Mr. Leroy, can we take a few minutes and ride down to the deadening? I swung by there late yesterday evenin' and I believe there's enough white showin' across that lightnin'-struck ridge to maybe get a bale offa it this next week."

The plantation owner motioned for him to get in. "Sure, c'mon. I'd might near forgotten about lookin' down there on that end of the field. You still want to use the boys to pick it?"

"If you say it's all right. I talked to 'em Sunday, and Buzz and Hump rode down there that afternoon on the hosses. They say it's beginnin' to pop open pretty good."

"Hell, Jose hasn't even got the press back together, has he? Can we gin it if we pick it?" Mr. Leroy asked as he turned onto the deadening turnrow.

"We'd have to jury-rig the tromper rack, but it'd be safe for just one bale right now. He finished gettin' the ram back together Friday, and they're settin' it up tomorrow, do you let 'em have the lift truck." Longmile pointed at a slightly higher ridge in the field. "See, now? Ain't that light land gettin' forced open quick?"

Mr. Leroy stopped the truck, and the two men walked across the cotton field rows, dew wetting their pants legs to the hips. On the indicated ridge, there was indeed a lot of the white fiber showing, the spread bolls beginning to turn from green to brown as the fluff dried within them. "We might have a bale open here,

Longmile," the owner opined. "Let's try it tomorrow. See can you find enough sacks; you know how they disappear over the winter and spring. I'll call Bubba Duncan to see if anybody else has a shot at the first bale. Have the boys out here soon as the dew's off, okay?"

"Yessir." The coach grinned. "And I'll get Jose on a stick about that tromper rack. Us'll take our best shot!"

The next day, the Barefoot Dodgers assembled at the barns, picking though a pile of cottonsacks that Longmile had been able to find. The six-foot-long sacks, with shoulder strap, would hold close to a hundred pounds apiece. Almost fifteen of them would have to be filled to provide enough cotton for a bale, once the ginning process had separated the seed from the fiber. Third and Luke rode up on horses, which would be used to transport the sacks from the middle of the field to the trailer, which Red had hooked to his father's pickup. Longmile appeared with a cotton scale and pee weight, which would be hung from a pole attached to one rear corner of the trailer.

"Everybody got a sack? Red, you got a water cooler in the truck? Now, remember: pick it clean! No snatchin' and comin' in to the scales with a sackfulla burrs. I'll knock a knot on your heads for that, 'cause it'll give me fits ginnin' it. Buzz, keep the preppin' around down to a minimum out there. Mr. Leroy says Goose Hollow's gonna make a run for it too, and this'll mean two thousand bucks toward new uniforms and expenses at the state tournament if we can beat 'em gettin' the first bale of the year."

"And then the regionals and then the national championship -- don't forget them," Hump reminded him.

"Let's cross one bridge at a time," his father responded. "Okay, load up in the pickup. I'm headed to the gin, 'cause we gotta full day's work to get ready to gin this bale. Good luck."

As Red's truck pulled away, Third dismounted and pulled a couple more sacks from the pile left. "Luke, I'm gonna help 'em pick a little, too, at least early, till some of 'em start gettin' full sacks for us to tote out."

"Hand me up one, too," his brother said. "I can't pull much, but maybe I can get enough to put us over the hump."

"It ain't gonna bother you, breathin' the lint?"

"Not early. I'll hafta quit before it gets hot. C'mon, I'll race you down there!" The brothers spurred their horses away from the barns toward the deadening, whooping.

TEAM *Barefoot Dodgers* RECORD   TEAM   RE

NO.	PLAYERS	B/A	POS INN	1	2	3	4	5	6
1	Willy B	RF				1-3			
	SUB. Brown Bro	RF	PH 6						
	SUB.								
2	Jimmy Lee	1B							
	SUB. Sherman	2B	4						
	SUB.			E3	61	RBZ			
3	Buzz	P	1B 4			F7		F7	
	SUB. III	1B	6						
	SUB.								
4	Hump	C			F8		E6		
	SUB.				RBZ		RBZ		
	SUB.								
5	Caleb	LF		6-4			F8		
	SUB.								
	SUB.								
6	Spider	SS		1-4-3			6-3		
	SUB.					RBZ			
	SUB.								
7	Rafe	CF	P 4		5-3	3-4			
	SUB. Hay-Sue	CF	4						
	SUB.								
8	Junior	3B		F9	4-3	4			
	SUB. Luke		PH 5						
	SUB. Red	3B	P 5						
9	Blue Daddy	2B			K				
	SUB. Wilbur 4th	2B	P 6			Z RBZ			
	SUB.								
	SUB.								
	SUB.								
Coach - Longmile									
	SUB.								
	SUB.								
UMPIRE Uncle Eb				4 3	3 2	1 1	1 0		
UMPIRE				LOB	LOB	LOB	LOB	LOB	LOB
UMPIRE				E	E	E	E	E	E
SCORER				B/P	B/P				

Chapter Nine

"White boy can't pick no cotton," Willy B declared, as Third and Luke slid from their horses' backs and pulled their sacks down.

"Black boy can't ride no horse," Luke rejoined. "We just gonna help out for a little while, till y'all get a sack or two full."

Hump was the shortest Dodger, and therefore the most comfortable in the field. "Y'all gonna get tired of stoopin' over 'fore this day's out. Liable to need them hosses to drag Buzz and Spider outa the field, they gonna be so sore."

The captain's long fingers were nimbly gathering the white locks and stuffing them into the sack. "Looks like the tallest guys would get to ride the hosses, don't it. Howcome you say a black boy can't ride, Luke? I can wrap my ole long legs 'round that filly and do better'n you, I betcha."

"You ain't ever seen a black movie cowboy, have you?" Third asked.

"Betcha I can outride you any day of the week and twice on Sundays!" Sherman snorted. "Ain't nothin' to ridin' a hoss, 'cept hangin' on."

"Well, really, how come then you never see black cowboys in the movies?" Red wanted to know. "There's lots of Indians, lots of Mexicans, but never a black in the picture shows. Y'all must can't ride good."

Spider stood from between the two rows he was picking and stretched his back. "You sho' right 'bout my back, Hump," he grimaced. "I'm gonna get me some knee pads tomorrow and crawl 'tween these rows."

"How long will it take us to get a bale?" Blue Daddy asked.

"Just pickin' mostly across this ridge, we oughta get it

tomorrow, if it's here," Rafe estimated. "Get it today if y'all shut up and pick, instead of talkin' 'bout bein' cowboys."

"I don't care nothin' 'bout them hosses," Junior declared. "Keep them things away from me! I saw a feller at a rodeo in Atlanta one time get bucked off and stomped on, and they carried him to the graveyard when that bronc was through with 'im."

Hump agreed emphatically. "That ole mule sho' messed me up for life. Ain't no tellin' how far I could hit a baseball if I had a good shoulder."

Buzz stood and stretched as Spider had. "Shoot, me and Third always thought the mule come off worst in that match. That ole swayback sonuvagun wasn't good for nothin' but pullin' water furrows after you'd ridden 'im for awhile. Besides, I figure you couldn't hit the broadside of the barn, 'cept for havin' that crooked shoulder. Pitcher sees you comin' up to bat, he just natcherly feels sorry for you, and lets up."

"Ole Pot musta sure felt sorry for 'im last weekend, then, 'cause that's the only way he'da beat me in that Home Run Derby," Luke noted.

"You wish!" Hump joked. "Here, Luke, be careful. You look like you're beginnin' to get a little red in the face."

"Luke, do us a favor," Caleb suggested. "How 'bout ridin' back to the truck and bring that water jug? Sun's fixin' to start burnin' now. Play cowboy for a while and get us some water."

The CF Kid stood and slipped out of his sack strap. "Gladly. It's kinda close down between these rows. Here, Third. Take what's in my sack. Anybody wanta send one back yet?" It was obvious that no one had more than a quarter of a sack. "Heck, I got as much as you, Willy B; white boys can too pick cotton! Don't you wish you could ride?" He dodged a green cotton boll aimed at him, then took off down the row in a brief spurt to get out of the range of another barrage. "Hey, don't make me run!"

he laughed. He walked back and mounted his pony. "Hi-yo, Silver!" he mocked. "See y'all in a while."

Hey-Sue seldom spoke, but now he directed a question at Third. "What ees the wrong with Luke? He can no take thees heat or run."

Third soberly replied, "He's got a lung disease called Cystic Fibrosis, Hey-Sue. His sweat glands don't work like yours and mine, and he gets too hot too quick. Plus, he's got a lot of congestion in his lungs. It's usually worse in the wintertime."

"Will he no get better?"

"He's better this summer than I think I've seen him in years, right, Buzz? But unless the docs find some cure for it, naw, chances are he won't get all right."

Buzz nodded agreement, "He had a good winter, and it's been good for him this summer. It comes and goes."

"Whatcha mean, he won't get all right?" Junior asked. "He'll grow out of it eventually, won't he?"

"Talk about somethin' else," Red growled, savagely jerking bolls from the plant before him.

"No snatchin'," Hump reminded him.

Third shook his head. "Junior, Hey-Sue, Blue: y'all ain't been here long. Luke's lucky to have made it to his age, accordin' to the statistics. That's why we watch him close, those of us who were raised here. We take it day by day. Y'all just help us keep an eye on 'im, okay? He's not bad to do more than he should, but sometimes it slips up on 'im."

"You mean...?" Blue Daddy ventured.

"Yeah. Pick cotton." Hump ordered.

By the end of the day, the Dodgers had accumulated just over a thousand pounds of cotton, Red's weigh-in tally indicated. Hump was high man, and Hey-Sue was low man, not counting Luke, Third, and Wilber. The towhead had left for an American

Legion game of his own after lunch, and Mr. Leroy had come to pick Wilber up soon after that, with the news that one of his children had stepped on a nail and needed to visit the doctor.

"Man! Can you imagine havin' chillen and all that?" Luke shook his head from his perch on the pony.

Blue Daddy stood and rubbed his eyes. "Yeah, I can," he mused, to everyone's laughter.

"Uh-huh. You'da minded your business, we'd been in Atlanta playin' in a rock and roll band now, 'steada pickin' cotton for some white boy on horseback! Massa, don't whup me, please! It wuz mah brother what done it!" Junior mocked.

"I got them weddin' bell blues," crooned Rafe, "from my head to my shoes...."

"That ain't funny, you guys! I'da made my second million by now, wasn't for that lttle Jessie May," Blue declared.

Chapter Ten

Buzz and Sherman paid a casual visit to the latter's cousin who lived in Goose Hollow that evening, learning that their rivals intended to begin picking the next day, on a similar light ridge. The cousin did not know that Brownspur had begun a run for the first bale, nor did the two Dodgers reveal that. "They'll find out soon enough," Sherman said as they got in Buzz's car to return to Brownspur.

"Aw, man, if Longmile and Jose get that gin cranked up, we got it knocked!" Buzz chortled.

The Dodgers assembled early, and were in the field before the dew had finished drying. By just after one o'clock, they heard the "Chuff! Chuff! Chuff!" of the huge cotton gin diesel engine cranking off for the first time since the winter ginning had finished. Caleb stood, holding up his crossed fingers. "Chuff! Chuff! Chuff, chuff, chuff...." the sound continued. Hump and Rafe cheered. Red put his fingers in his mouth and whistled piercingly.

"Let's weigh up right quick, and I'll run it over there," he instructed. Their combined total was four hundred pounds. "It's a little damp in the bottom of the sacks," Red noted as he emptied the first two. "Maybe we ought to get another couple hundred. I'll carry this on over, 'cause Longmile will be startin' all the machinery up slow." He and Spider finished dumping the sacks, and the trailer sped away as the remaining Dodgers returned to the ridge.

In just over an hour, Red reappeared without the trailer, tooting the horn. Third and Luke gathered all the sacks on their mounts, and trotted to meet the truck. The sacks were thrown in the pickup bed, and all the boys jumped in. Back at the gin, another 120 pounds was added to the trailer, for a total of nearly 1600 pounds of seed cotton. Jose Melendez allowed Caleb, Rafe, Buzz, and Sherman to "pull the ties," as the wide steel bands holding the bale of lint together were called, while he and Longmile carefully watched the tromper rack press the lint into the oblong bale that proved to weigh 526 pounds. Mr. Leroy backed his pickup to the concrete bale platform, and Spider wheeled the bale into the bed on the dolly. The truck pulled up, Longmile slammed the tailgate shut, and yelled, "Take 'er away!"

"Hop in!" Mr. Leroy invited. He meant Longmile, but the Barefoot Dodgers took it as an en masse invitation. At five minutes until five o'clock, Bubba Duncan heard a blaring horn in front of his cotton brokerage, and opened the door to find not only the first cotton bale of the year, but fourteen Barefoot Dodgers, Wilber having stayed home with his wounded child. The front of the pickup jutted upward, with all the weight in the back of it. "Did we get it?!" Leroy Alexander yelled to his cotton buyer. "The First Bale?"

Duncan grinned, "You got it! Lemme call the paper and see can I get a reporter down here. I just had a call from Goose Hollow, sayin' they were crankin' up their gin, but it's gonna be too late. Back up here and let's unload and weigh it." He pulled a handful of lint from the bale and held it up to the sunlight. "Nice. You want the check made out to you, or a tenant, Leroy?"

"Neither one. Make it out to the Barefoot Dodgers, Bubba!"

"The who? Oh, yeah, that's y'all's baseball team, isn't it? That who picked it?"

"Yessir!" Buzz declared proudly. "The Barefoot Dodgers, goin' to be the champs this year!"

"That so?"

"Absolutely. We nearly took the state last year, and we're gonna go all the way this year," Rafe boasted.

Duncan motioned Mr. Leroy to the side as the boys unloaded the bale from the truck. "They that good, Leroy? Sure 'nuff?"

"Could be, Bubba. They're solid. I told 'em if they got the First Bale, they could use all the money for uniforms and travel expenses, if they won the tournaments. They're in some kind of league that's gonna have a national championship."

"Hey, this is gonna be some kind of good publicity for me! Lemme go call the paper. You mind if I use that story? It's a whole lot better than the usual First Bale of the Year story."

"Well...that's a lotta sugar for a nickel, Bubba. Tell you what. You can use the team for your good publicity, but then if they win the state championship, you gotta put up another...oh, say, five hundred bucks."

"But then I get to put 'em on teevee and everything, right?"

"That's included. Deal?" Mr. Leroy stuck out his hand.

Duncan shook. "Say, if they win the state, reckon I could buy 'em uniforms with Duncan Cotton Company on 'em?"

Mr. Leroy shook his head. "Nope. They'll be wearin' uniforms sayin' Barefoot Dodgers. Period. Call your reporter, Bubba, and get ready to cough up another halfa grand soon!"

TEAM *Barefoot Dodgers*   RECORD   TEAM   RE

NO.	PLAYERS	B/A	POS/INN	1	2	3	4	5	6
1	Willy B	RF				1-3	F9		
	SUB. Brown Sue	RF	A4/6						
	SUB.								
2	Jimmy Lee	1B							
	SUB. Sherman	2B	4			1			
	SUB.			E3	61	RBI			
3	Buzz	P	10/4			F7	F7		
	SUB. III	1B	6						
	SUB.								
4	HUMP	C			F8		E6		
	SUB.								
	SUB.				RBI		RBI		
5	Caleb	LF		6-4			F8		
	SUB.								
	SUB.								
6	Spider	SS		6-4-3			6-3		
	SUB.					RBI			
	SUB.								
7	RAFE	CF/P	4		5-3	3-4			
	SUB. Hay-Sue	CF	4						
	SUB.								
8	Junior	3B		F9	4-3	K			
	SUB. Luke		PR5						
	SUB. Red	3B	PR5						
9	Blue Daddy	2B		K					
	SUB. Wilbur 4th	2B	P6			2 RBI			
	SUB.								
	SUB.								
	SUB.								
	Coach - Longmile								
	SUB.								
	SUB.								
UMPIRE *Uncle Eb*				R 4 3 H	R 3 2 H	R 1 1 H	R 1 0 H	R H	R
UMPIRE				LOB 1 / ER	LOB 2 / ER	LOB 1 / ER	LOB 1 / ER	LOB / ER	LOB
UMPIRE				E	E	E	E	E	E
SCORER				D/P		D/P			

60   *The Barefoot Dodgers*

Chapter Eleven

It showered that night, so there was no early work on the plantation, except for Mr. Wood's men at the shop and the gin crew. Following a call from Bubba Duncan, Mr. Leroy sent Third out to gather the Barefoot Dodgers at the commissary. The big state daily newspaper was sending a reporter and photographer up to cover the story of the baseball team picking the first bale. Longmile also took advantage of the gathering to get the owner to call Chief McMaster, who had the local sporting goods operation, and have samples and catalogues of uniforms shown to the team. The sporting goods man got there first.

"Mankind!" Buzz punched Hump. "We can get first-class uniforms for the whole team for less'n fifteen hundred bucks!"

"Not countin' cleats, yeah."

Chief heard the comment. "I'll throw in a dozen sets of cleats for half the retail price, if y'all buy at least a dozen uniforms," he offered.

Mr. Leroy was doing the tallying, and looked up. "Done!" he exclaimed. "Longmile, that's too good a deal to pass up. Even if some of the boys have cleats already, these will belong to the team. Third, take a tablet and write down everybody's shoe size and give it to Chief."

"Mr. Leroy, we ain't got but eleven players," Longmile reminded him.

"Then get a uniform for yourself; order one for your scorekeeper, if you want. That's just too good to let go by. Hell, you still ain't spent much more'n fifteen hundred bucks, like Buzz said."

"What about an emblem?" Chief asked. "You got the name on the shirts free, and you get an emblem on the caps, too."

"Luke, how about drawin' us up something?" Longmile suggested. The CF Kid was a pretty good artist. "Buzz, you and Hump work with him on it. Sketch out a few samples and Mr. Leroy and I will approve one. How quick you need it, Mr. Chief?"

"Aw, a week or so will be okay. We put the emblems on at our shop, so it isn't something I have to send off. Make it about three inches square or smaller, Luke, okay?"

"Yessir," Luke grinned.

McMaster was just leaving with his order when the reporter and photographer drove up. The Barefoot Dodgers posed on the catchpen fence for group pictures, and then the reporter asked for four members to interview inside. Longmile designated Buzz, Hump, Rafe, and Spider, and dismissed the rest of the team. "Be back up here around five for practice," he reminded them.

"Well, what y'all wanta do, burn the haybarn again?" Willy B asked.

"I'd just as soon find some other kinda fun this afternoon," Junior opined. "Wanta go down to the swimmin' hole?"

Sherman pointed toward the pasture. "Naw. Yonder's a chance to make Luke eat his words from the other day. How much you wanta bet I can ride that colt, Luke?"

Third warned, "Sherman, that colt ain't ever been broke yet. I wouldn't mess with him."

"He ain't even had a saddle on his back," Luke pointed out.

"Man, a black cowboy don't need no saddle! Help me get a bridle on that sucker, and I'll ride him to kingdom come,"Sherman boasted. "You wanta ride too, Jimmy Lee?"

"I ain't gonna be first, is all," was the answer. "If you bust the meanness outa him, I'll go second, I reckon."

"Y'all better not mess with that colt until Mr. Leroy says it's okay," Red Wood protested. "I tried him two weeks ago, and he laid me flat on my back in the catch pen, and Mr. Leroy told me not to mess with him any more. He's too green."

"Ain't nothing too green for no black cowboy," Blue sang. "How 'bout a song: 'Blue Daddy, the Brownspur Black Cowboy on the Green Bronc'! Lemme get Rafe's new guitar."

"I ain't gettin' on no horse, green or black," his brother growled.

Brown Brother offered, "You want me to run to the haybarn for a bridle, Sherman?"

"Yeah, go ahead. C'mon, you guys, help me round that colt up. Luke, you mind holdin' the catchpen gate open while we run him in there?"

"Okay, but you cruisin' for a bruisin'," the CF Kid warned.

"Eef Sherman cannot ride heem, I weel," Hey-Sue stated calmly.

The others looked strangely at him. "You a bronco buster?" said Caleb dubiously.

"We catch and break wild hosses een Mexico, my family. I have done many busting broncos. Eef you like, I weel go first."

"No way! It's bad enough bein' talked down to by Luke. C'mon, let's run him into the catchpen, y'all."

The boys rounded up the colt while Brown Brother returned with a bridle. Sherman still vowed to ride the horse without a saddle, though both Red and Hey-Sue warned against it. "I'm gonna show y'all how a black cowboy does it!" he declared.

Third and Caleb held the colt next to the fence, while Sherman carefully climbed to the top rail. Third pulled the horse's head to one side, and Sherman jumped aboard, grabbing the reins. Boys scattered to climb the rails as the bucking started.

"Ride 'im, cowboy!" yelled Jimmy Lee.

"Hold on!" called Luke.

"Keep hees head op!" Hey-Sue warned.

"Watch out for the fence!"

"Lock your knees!"

Sherman was getting more advice than he needed, or had time to listen to. The crowhopping, sunfishing pony bounced off the fence on one gyration, and the boys saw Sherman wince with pain. The bronc switched ends in the air, and his rider flew head over heels, landing on his back in the center of the catchpen. Caleb and Jimmy Lee ran to protect their fallen comrade as Hey-Sue and Third tried to catch the colt. Finally, the Mexican lad managed to grab the reins and stop the horse at the fence.

"You got him okay?" Third asked, getting a nod in reply.

Sherman was rocking and moaning, holding his ankle in the center of a group of teammates. "Lemme see, black cowboy," Caleb demanded, trying to straighten out the injured leg.

"Yaaahhhhh! Quit, dammit!" Sherman screamed. The foot was bent at a peculiar angle. Third knelt down to examine it.

"That sucker's broke, I betcha," was his prognosis.

"Man, naw!" Willy B protested.

"Looks like it," Caleb declared sourly. "Black cowboy, you sho' done messed up this time!"

"Help me up," demanded Sherman.

"No way!" Third was firm. "Me and Buzz helped Hump back up when he got thrown off that mule years ago. You want an ankle like his shoulder? You hold still and lemme get Daddy." He ran for the commissary.

The interview was just breaking up, and Third beckoned Mr. Leroy off to one side. "Daddy, Sherman tried to ride that colt, and got bucked off. I think his ankle is broken -- bad."

"Dad-gummit! I told Red just a few days ago to leave that colt alone! Where is he?"

"Yessir, Red told us that and tried to warn him off, but wouldn't nothing do but he was gonna ride it. We better get him in to the doctor. Everybody's in the catchpen."

The owner sighed, "Well, it coulda been worse, I guess. I got a busted wrist from the same thing when I was y'all's age. Let those newspaper folks get outa here before you say anything to Longmile and the rest. I'll go look at Sherman. When they leave, back my truck up to the catchpen gate."

As the newspapermen pulled away, the Barefoot Dodgers' coach, captain, and their important-feeling mates turned to see Mr. Leroy's pickup pulling away from the catchpen with several Dodgers in the back. Third stopped next to them, and they saw Sherman lying on a pile of cotton sacks, groaning. "Ankle's broke, Longmile," Mr. Leroy announced. "Hop in back here and some of you hold him steady while I drive. Luke, run call the doctor and tell him to get ready. We're bringing him a customer."

Buzz leaned over the injured youngster. "What the heck were you doin'?"

Willy B answered, "This here's the black cowboy of Brownspur, Buzz. You wanta ask him now why there ain't no black cowboys in the picture shows?"

Third had relinquished the steering wheel to his father, and the truck pulled away, swung into the county road, and accelerated toward town, leaving the rest of the boys standing in front of the commissary. "What're we gonna....?" Hump's question was interrupted by a shout from the catchpen.

Jimmy Lee, Red, and Junior were still perched on the rails. "Ride 'im, cowboy! Do it! Hang on!" they yelled. The Dodgers ran for the fence.

Hey-Sue sat atop the bucking, wild-eyed colt, swaying from side to side with the horse's leaps. Another sunfish maneuver into the fence failed to dislodge the Mexican, though he kicked his leg on that side high enough that it wasn't slammed against the rail. Round and around the catchpen the colt bucked, but it could not unseat the rider. Finally, the pony stopped, trembling, then began a jerky trot, guided in a circle by Hey-Sue, who reined in next to Jimmy Lee. "You next?" the Mexican grinned.

"Not none-a me, dude. I ain't no black cowboy, and I ain't lookin' to be in no movie!" But there was new respect in his eyes, as well as the others', for the young brown cowboy.

Chapter Twelve

The season had come down to its final regular season week, and the Barefoot Dodgers, at 29-9, had the best record in the northwest section of the state, except for a team for up near the Tennessee state line that the Dodgers had never played before, the Moon Lake Moonmen. The Moonmen played most of their games with teams in the Memphis/West Memphis area, and seldom traveled as far south as Brownspur. The state tournament was a double-elimination affair involving the best teams from the four corners of Mississippi, and the league officials had decreed a three-game series between the Dodgers and the Moonmen, as the best in the northwest. Brownspur was to host the first game, with the final two to be played at Moon Lake two days later.

On Wednesday before the scheduled Brownspur game, Abner Johnson received the sad news that his mother had passed away in Atlanta. Without a word to anyone but Mr. Leroy, the Johnsons packed up and left for the funeral -- an eight-hour drive away. Longmile learned on Thursday that his second and third basemen would probably not return before Sunday. He made a call to the Moon Lake coach, Bones Reeder.

"Coach, I gotta bad situation here. One of my boys broke an ankle, and two others are in Atlanta for a funeral. Could we possibly postpone the game a couple of days?"

The Moonmen mentor was reluctant. "Longmile, I don't wanta do that. One of my best players has to report to college on Sunday, so Saturday is the only day I can use one of my aces. You ain't gotta substitute you can use?"

"Well, you'll have to accomodate me, 'cause I got two or three white boys been practicin' with us and they're all I got to substitute. That okay with you?"

"You ain't gotta start more'n one, do you?"

"Not unless somebody else gets hurt. They're from here on the place -- matter of fact, they're even on my roster, you wanta know the truth. One of 'em pitches, but I wouldn't use him there for this game. That okay?"

"Right age? And they ain't ringers, are they?"

"Oh, yeah," the Dodger coach assured his counterpart. "They're the right age, all in high school, but only one plays high school baseball. I ain't ringin' in no college All-American on y'all, I promise."

Reeder was casual in his reply. "Sure, I'll accomodate you on this; who knows, you might have to accomodate me on a player sometime. Never can tell."

"Thanks, coach. See you day after tomorrow."

Longmile asked Third and Red to be prepared to play in that first game. "I can't start but one of you, and if Junior or Blue get back in time, of course I'd play them. But I don't look for them back, so be ready."

"Lookin' forward to it," Red spoke for both of the boys.

Saturday, the Moon Lake team arrived just before game time, and hurriedly loosened up along the left field line. Bones Reeder shook Longmile's hand as he handed him the lineup card. "Sorry we was runnin' late, coach. Lotta traffic. Your boys get back from the funeral?"

"Naw, 'fraid not. I'll be startin' a white boy in the infield. Won't bother any of your kids, will it?"

"Uh-uh. I told 'em we'd be pretty hang loose for this first game. Well, lemme give my boys infield. Good luck."

Buzz was to start pitching, so he and Hump were warming up down the right field line while Longmile met with his team. "Okay, guys, we can whup this bunch. Jimmy Lee, you be more comfortable at third or first? I can play either Third or Red today.

Make y'all any difference?"

Jimmy Lee scratched his head contemplatively. "We been talkin' it over, coach. Third's a better fielder than I am at first, and a better hitter than Red. I do okay on third, long as I can fudge over toward the hole. If they start buntin' we might have to change, since I throw lefty, but our strongest lineup will be with Third on first."

Longmile nodded agreement. "That okay with you, Red? Third?" He got nods in reply. "Okay, guys, let's eat their lunch! Go git 'em!"

As the Dodgers took the field, Spider noted to Buzz, "You know, their emblems do look like Moon Pies. We sho'nuff oughta eat these guys' lunch!"

"Moon Pies for lunch!" was the Dodgers' cry as the infielders tossed the ball around. Luke sketched a bare foot crushing a Moon Pie on the scorebook, causing Brown Brother to laugh hysterically.

"Y'all better take these guys seriously," warned Longmile.

The first Moonman singled back through the box, but two pitches later Spider got a perfect double play ball, flipped it to Wilber, who relayed to Third. The number three hitter popped up to Jimmy Lee. "Moon Pies for lunch!" yelled the Barefoot Dodgers, coming in to take their turn at bat, a laughing, joking, confident bunch. Longmile scowled.

Willy B led off, stepping into the box with a grin. The Moonman pitcher had warmed up down the left field line, and did not take the mound until Uncle Eb called "Play Ball!" Bones Reeder accompanied his hurler to the mound, talking earnestly, and held his hand out to take the warmup jacket back to the dugout. Willy B stepped into the box, waggling his bat.

"Hey! What's goin' on?" Luke exclaimed, pointing toward the mound. The Dodgers followed his questioning look.

The Moon Lake pitcher had removed the jacket while facing away from the Dodger bench. Now the hurler removed the baseball cap and shook out two long pigtails which had been concealed. Turning to face Willy B, the Moonman revealed a well-filled uniform shirt. "A girl!" Brown Brother declared. Willy B was still ogling, with his bat on his shoulder, when the first pitch sailed over for a perfect strike.

"Hey, time!" Longmile called as his batter stepped out of the box in confusion. Uncle Eb held up his hand as both coaches advanced to the plate. "That's a girl, Bones!" Longmile pointed out.

"You got that right, coach. What's the problem?" was the grinning rejoinder.

Willy B looked at the catcher, who was laughing behind the mask. "This a joke, buddy?"

"That first pitch look like a joke? You ain't laughin' now, are you, Moon Pie eater!"

"Bones, you can't play no girl!" Longmile declared. "This is a boy's game!"

"It don't say that nowhere in the rules, Longmile," the opposing coach said calmly. "It says that 'participants' must be between the ages of fifteen and nineteen, and if they reach their twentieth birthday before August 15, they can't play that summer. That's all it says. But I told you I might want an accomodation in return for you playin' your white boy. Gracie's got a basketball scholarship to Ole Miss, and gotta report tomorrow, and today's the only day she can play for us."

"But...but...she's a girl!"

"A girl who can chunk the hell out of a baseball. She don't hit too well, but she won six games pitchin' this year."

"My boys can't hit against no girl. They'd feel un-American! It ain't Christian!"

The Barefoot Dodgers

"I'll guarantee you they ain't gonna hit well against Gracie, but it ain't gonna be because it's against their religion. What about it, Ump?"

Uncle Eb had his rule book out, and shrugged. "He's right, Longmile. Let's play ball. Batter up!"

"Well, I never....Bones, you been playin' her all year?"

The Moon Lake coach laughed. "She's won six games, like I said, Longmile. She don't dress out 'cept when she's pitchin'. We call her Amazin' Gracie; I think you'll see why."

"Play ball!" demanded Uncle Eb, motioning the two coaches from the field of play.

"Uncle Eb, I got to bat against a GIRL?!" Willy B asked plaintively.

"And you awready got one strike against you," noted the ump.

Willy B looked at another strike in wonder, then cleanly missed a curve that broke outside. "Yer out!" called Uncle Eb.

It was apparent that the right fielder didn't even want to return to the Dodger bench, where his mates were laughing. Spider had to take the bat from him. "She got curves, Willy B?" the shortstop cackled.

But Spider's mirth was short-lived. Uncle Eb called a curve on the outside corner a strike, then a fast ball only got a glance. "She got pretty good speed," Spider allowed, stepping out to rub dirt on his hands.

"That's why we call her Amazin' Gracie," agreed the grinning catcher. "And you're right -- she does have a curve or two!" He was still laughing when Spider took another curve, then protested in disbelief when Uncle Eb called it the third strike.

"If she was a boy, you'da called that a ball outside!" declared Spider. "C'mon, Uncle Eb!"

"Batter's out! Batter up!" the umpire called.

Buzz passed a grumbling Spider on his way to bat. "What's she got, man?" the lanky captain asked.

"Got the ump in her pocket," his teammate growled.

Buzz was the first Dodger to get wood on the ball, popping up to deep short. "How 'bout a bite-a Moon Pie, boys?" the catcher mocked in falsetto. The Moon Lake bench jeered the Dodger captain and his mates as they took the field again.

Chapter Thirteen

Shaken, Buzz walked the Moonman cleanup, then gave up a double that plated him. Spider booted an easy grounder, trying to look the runner back before he gloved the ball. With runners at the corners, Buzz bore down and struck out the next batter, and the eight hitter fouled out to Hump. With two out and two on, Amazin' Gracie stepped in, crowding the plate. "Ain't she a little close, Ump? One-a her things is hangin' over the plate!" Hump asked.

"Time!" called Uncle Eb. "Son, you can't say stuff like that, or I'll throw you outa this game so fast...."

Longmile rushed the plate, interrupting him. "What's wrong! What'd he say, Ump?"

"He said one-a my...my...that parta me was hangin' out over the plate!" the offended batter screeched. "I've never...."

"Pigtails! Pigtails! That's all I meant!" Hump protested.

"What else you thought he was talkin' about, Uncle Eb? Huh?" Longmile demanded. "Shoot, I could see her pigtail in the strike zone from where I was at! She can't stand on toppa home!"

"He meant my...."

"Hush up, batter! You sure you was talkin' about pigtails, Hump?" the old man asked suspiciously. Getting a wide-eyed nod in return, he motioned toward the mound with his left while motioning Longmile back toward the bench with his right. "Play ball!" he called. The Moonman coach stood up from the bench.

"Hey, you can't let him get away with insultin' my...."

"HUSH!!" the umpire silenced Bones Reeder. "PLAY BALL!!"

Buzz walked her on four pitches, to load the bases. The

leadoff sliced a shot down the line in right, two runs scored, and the relay to Jimmy Lee was in time, but he dodged the sliding runner and she was safe under his tag, Uncle Eb right on top of the play to make the call.

Amazin' Gracie jumped to her feet calling time. "Did you see where he tagged me?! Throw 'im out, Ump!" The Moonman coach rushed up too.

"You gonna let him get away with that? C'mon, Ump! You saw where he tagged my runner!"

Jimmy Lee was almost in tears. "I never did! I just swiped at her, Uncle Eb. I didn't mean to touch her...."

The elderly umpire was fed up. "Lissen! She plays with boys, she plays by the same rules as boys! Dad-gummit! Quit hollerin' and PLAY BALL!!"

A rattled Buzz walked the next hitter, but Wilber made a nice diving catch of a low liner to retire the side with no more damage. "C'mon, guys!" Luke encouraged as the Dodgers came in down by three runs. "Surely y'all can hit this girl!"

Hump strode resolutely to the batter's box and took his stance. Longmile saw his son's concentration break as the pitcher went into her windup. "Stee-rike one!" bawled Uncle Eb.

Once again, Longmile noted that Hump's normally aggressive mood was strangely altered as the pitcher leaned in to get the sign. He swung belatedly at a changeup that was over his head. "Time!" called Longmile, beckoning his son to meet him halfway. "What the heck's wrong with you, boy?" he demanded.

"Aw, Daddy, I...I guess it's just hittin' against a girl."

"Well, durnit, forget she's a girl! Watch the durn BALL!"

Longmile wasn't sat down good before Uncle Eb called the third strike on a befuddled Hump. As the catcher began to replace his shin guards, he mumbled to Buzz, too low for anyone else to hear, "Man, she's got her shirt unbuttoned partway! Every time she bends over to get the signal....Woo-wee!"

"Woo-wee from sixty feet? C'mon, Hump! Get it together!"

"Hey, I noticed you ain't put good wood on the ball."

Caleb also took a called third strike, shaking his head. Buzz and Hump cornered him back on the bench. "What's wrong, son? You acted like you never saw the ball. Whatcha lookin' at up there, huh?"

The seldom-spoken left fielder shook his head. "Gonna be tough to hit her! Woo-wee!"

Hump nodded at Buzz. "From sixty feet, see there?"

Third grounded to short. Buzz got hit hard in the third, but also got a great play from Willy B on a ball that the runner didn't tag on and was doubled up after an almost impossible catch. Though Jimmy Lee errored on a grounder and then threw wild to first, the Dodgers escaped with no runs being scored against them. Longmile met them at the first base coaching box as they trotted in. "What's got into you guys? You playin' like you're sleepwalkin'! Get some pep! Get some hits!"

Jimmy Lee opened the bottom of the third with a beautiful drag bunt, but slowed and dodged out of the baseline when the pitcher fielded the ball. Longmile protested interference, but Uncle Eb correctly pointed out that Amazin' Gracie had never made contact with the runner -- since he had run out of the baseline.

Rafe too obviously fell for the open shirtfront trick that had distracted Caleb and Hump, and struck out. Wilber, the oldest and only married Dodger, got good wood on the ball, but it was a line shot back to the mound, gloved by Amazin' Gracie. The Barefoot Dodgers had batted around without a hit; indeed, with only four of them putting the ball in play -- against a girl!

"C'mon, guys," Brown Brother begged, but his plea fell on deaf ears. By the sixth inning, the Dodgers were behind by five runs, and had managed only one hit, a single by Wilber. "We gotta get some hits!" the team mascot declared, but there seemed little optimism along the bench.

Sherman, seated in a wheel chair behind the catchpen fence, borrowed four bits from Mr. Leroy and paid his two little brothers to slip across the Dog and let out the Rally Pigs. Even their appearance on the field failed to cheer the team. "That Amazin' Gracie's a witch herself," Willy B declared. "Even the Witch Doctor couldn't hit her curves!"

Rafe took the mound in the seventh, and set the Moonmen down in order, to start a little chatter among his mates. Heartened, he then led off with a double, and Wilber took an inside curve for the team, the ball hitting him just above the knee. Willy B sacrificed to move the runners up, and Spider beat out a grounder to third when the throw went home, Rafe scrambling back safely to third. Buzz, who had been angry the whole game, took a fastball down the line in left, clearing the bases and stopping at second. "Aw right!" the captain yelled. "Now we got her number!"

But Hump didn't, focusing on the pitcher's loosely buttoned shirt again and fouling out. "Two down, now. Watch 'em close," Longmile called to Caleb.

The left fielder stepped into the box, then jerked his head back and stepped out. "What'd you say?" he asked his coach disbelievingly.

Longmile walked halfway down the line, clapping his hands. "I said two down! Watch 'em over close. Make 'em be...."

"Time, Mister Ump!" Caleb called. "Make her button up."

"Do what?" Uncle Eb and the catcher echoed. Bones Reeder started up from the bench, and Longmile stalked down the line.

The Barefoot Dodgers

"Make her button her shirt," Caleb demanded. "The rule book says every player gotta have their shirts buttoned and shirt tails stuffed in. She ain't buttoned up. Make her."

Amazin' Gracie's infielders grinned, but the coach protested. "Aw, Ump, it's hot out here. Ain't no harm in a player havin' their shirt undone a little. It's...."

"Boy's right, Coach. That's what the rule book says. She's gotta button up if an opposin' team says so. Button up your shirt, Pitch," he called.

"Aw, Ump, I ain't gotta...." the pitcher began to argue.

"BUTTON UP AND PLAY BALL!" the umpire ordered.

Caleb walked on four pitches, all inside, two of them close enough to put him in the dirt on his back. Longmile protested that his hitter was being thrown at, but Caleb took his base unruffled. Third stepped from the on-deck circle.

"Time!" Longmile called, trotting to the bench and beckoning to his scorekeeper. He curled an arm around Luke's shoulders. "Say, Luke, I don't know what this girl's been doin' to these dummies, but can you hit her? Can you put one out on her?"

Brown Brother had also horned in on the conference. "Can Luke hit her? Luke can hit anybody, coach!"

Luke was somewhat mystified himself. "Sure I can hit her, Longmile. So what?"

"We gotta have somebody put some confidence back in our guys. If the CF Kid can swat the hell outa one, it might be just what they need to snap 'em out of it. Look, you pinch hit for Third, and get these two runs in. Don't try to run yourself -- just knock it far enough to get down to first. I'll put Red in to pinch run for you and play third, then move Jimmy Lee to first. But if they see you hit her, it'll give the rest some confidence. Okay?"

"Sure. Here, Brown Brother, take the scorebook."

"Ump, I gotta substitute," Longmile called, giving Luke time to take some practice swings while he reported the change.

Reeder came to the plate. "Thought you wasn't goin' to play but one white boy, Longmile?"

"Just one atta time, Bones. You gotta problem with that? I dressed out all three; I just figured to give 'em all a chance to play, okay?"

The Moonman coach looked at the blonde, well-built Third, and considered his younger brother, who was slighter of build and was sniffing from a pocket oxygen inhaler. "Well, okay, I guess. Hey, Ump, lemme get them hogs run outa the corner of right field." Uncle Eb nodded, and Luke took advantage of the time to swing two bats around his head. Finally the Rally Pigs were behind the haybarn and the Moonmen outfielders in position.

"Play ball," Uncle Eb called, rather wearily.

Luke looked at a fast ball, passed up a curve that was just outside for a ball, and edged up in the box to rap another curve into the gap in left center. Buzz and Caleb scored easily, and Longmile almost had to tackle Luke, who trotted to first, but then obviously considered heading for second. The score was tied, and Bones came out to talk to Amazin' Gracie, who kicked the mound in disgust. Red came in to run for Luke, who walked off the field to the bench's "LUKE, LUKE, LUKE, LUKE" cadence.

Coach Reeder decided to leave his pitcher in, and Red led off the bag chattering. "Hey, Gracie, what's so amazin' now? Them curves ain't breakin' so hot now, huh? Button up, babe, button up!"

"Shut up, white boy!" the first sacker growled, holding the runner on.

"Button up! Button up!" needled Red, drawing a pickoff

throw, and scrambling back safely. "Oooo! Don't tag me there!" he screamed in falsetto, moving the Barefoot Dodger bench to raucous laughter.

"Peck, peck, peck! Don't touch that Red-headed peckerWood on his ole peckerWood! Button up, Gracie!" called the Dodgers.

Furious, the Moon Lake hurler whirled and fired to first again, but too high for the Moonman manning the bag. The throw sailed over the baseman's glove and Red was away, headed for second and rounding the bag. The right fielder tripped dodging one of the Rally Pigs, who were safely off the field of play, as was the ball. Red went to third without drawing a throw. "Peck, peck, peck, Gracie!" taunted the Dodger bench. Red led off, expecting the suicide squeeze with the drag-bunting expert Jimmy Lee at the plate. He promptly drew a throw that the third baseman had to leap for. "Peck, peck, peck!" called the bench, infuriating Amazin' Gracie. The redhead pantomimed shock at the too-late tag by the fielder. "Oooo! Don't touch that Red-headed peckerWood there!" yelled the Dodgers. "Button up, pitch!"

Jimmy Lee's drag bunt was perfect. Gracie was so occupied watching Red's lead from third that she was off balance and fell trying to field the bunt. Red scored without a throw, though the catcher half-heartedly blocked the plate, and the runner welcomed a semi-collision. Jimmy Lee was safe, also without a throw. Gracie wild-pitched him to second, walked Rafe, and Wilber teed off on a changeup, coming all the way around when the throw got by the third baseman. "BOOT! BOOT! BOOT! BOOT!" chanted the Dodgers at the error, and from over the catchpen fence sailed a pair of rubber boots. "BOOT! BOOT! BOOT!" laughed the fans.

Amazin' Gracie was lifted, but the Barefoot Dodgers were not finished. They scored six more runs before the dazed

Moonmen left Brownspur, and Wilber finished up for the save. Two days later, with the Johnson boys back, the Dodgers traveled to Moon Lake and clinched the northwest title, winning by the ten-run rule after five innings. Red and Third smuggled a Rally Pig in through a hole in the center field fence, and took credit for the victory. A third game was not needed, and the shoat was barbequed, so as to accompany the Dodgers to the state playoffs.

Chapter Fourteen

The Barefoot Dodgers' new uniforms arrived the week before the state tournament, and Longmile passed them out. "Y'all look like a baseball team now," Mr. Leroy complimented them. Luke's design of a black bare foot, toes seeming to grip a baseball, was emblazoned on the caps and left breast pocket of the shirts. Longmile had ordered an extra uniform for Luke, and Mr. Leroy had paid for extra shirts and caps for Third, Red, Hey-Sue, Uncle Eb, and Brown Brother. The tournament was to be played in Jackson, the capital and largest centrally-located city, and several umpires from a city league would help call the games, so Uncle Eb could serve as assistant coach in games he didn't have to call.

Bubba Duncan, true to his promise, had arranged for another newspaper article and a television interview with the Barefoot Dodgers in full uniform, together with the First Bale displayed at his brokerage. Several smaller area newspapers picked up on the story and also sent reporters to attend the press conference. Longmile was jittery. "Alla this publicity might go to these boys' heads, Mr. Leroy." he warned.

"Just remind them of Amazin' Gracie if that happens," was the reply.

The Saturday of the tournament was clear and hot, the humidity almost tangible. The Dodgers were used to this kind of weather -- as a matter of fact, welcomed it. Hump always claimed that Buzz's pitches had more movement on them during days with high humidity, and it was a valid theory. The lanky captain started the first game and advanced the Dodgers into the winner's bracket with a splendid two-hitter, throwing only eighty-four pitches. Hump had a solo homer in the second, and Jimmy Lee squeezed in Rafe for an insurance run in the seventh.

Rafe was a little wild to begin the second game, that afternoon, but a classy double play from Spider to Blue Daddy to Buzz got him out of a jam in the first, and he settled down. At one point he struck out five in a row. Back to back doubles by Caleb and Junior after a walk to Willy B produced two runs, and in the sixth Spider tripled with Buzz aboard, then came home on Blue's flyout to right. Longmile lifted Rafe for Wilber in the eighth, hoping to be able to use all his pitchers if needed the next day, and Wilber closed it out, giving up one run in the ninth before Junior snagged a liner over third and tagged the runner, who was going, for the final out.

The tension that night in the hotel room was almost unbearable. Longmile worried, "You guys are takin' this too seriously. Hang loose. We're in the winner's bracket now, and all we gotta do is win one of our next two. Go see a movie. Play cards. Loosen up. Don't blow our big chance by gettin' tight now! Remember Amazin' Gracie!"

Most of the Dodgers were congregated in Buzz and Hump's room when Third stuck his head in the door. "I come in? What's goin' on? One more's all it takes, guys!"

Buzz beckoned him in. "Yeah, we're close, Third. Kinda scary, really. We're country boys, but if we win this next game or the one after that, we'll be on teevee, in the papers, and be goin' to Birmingham for the regionals."

"That's what it's all about, right? After the regionals come the nationals, too. Hey, y'all are good -- face it!"

"There's gonna be major league scouts, national teevee, big magazine reporters, alla that kinda stuff if we win tomorrow," Hump declared. "That's a lotta pressure, Third. What if someone boots a ball? Even folks in New York City would know it!"

"Fame and fortune," agreed the towhead. "Everybody blows one now and then. But if somebody has a good game, like Buzz did yesterday, or if somebody makes a flashy play, like that double play ball Spider pulled out, they see that too. It's all part of the game."

"Bein' good's one thing, but bootin' one's another. Make a mistake, and the whole world's gonna see it," Rafe noted. "A bad play could mark you for life -- kill your one chance for the majors, maybe."

"Who was the losin' pitcher in the World Series first game year before last?" Third asked.

It threw the players off balance. "Heck, who played year before last? The Reds and the Orioles?" Willy B speculated.

"Naw, it was the Cards and.... I can't remember," Buzz said.

"Was it the...naw, that was three years ago," Hump scratched his head.

"That's my point," Third declared. "Y'all gotta think hard to come up with who even played a couple of years ago, much less a pitcher that gave up a gopher ball in the ninth. And that's the major leagues! Who's gonna remember even the winnin' pitcher in a black league's state championship game -- even next week? This is just a chance for the guys who show up good enough to play pro ball someday -- and nobody here is over nineteen years old! At this stage, it's just a fun game; a chance to make a helluva memory before you get old and married, like Wilber."

Wilber agreed. "Y'all listen to Third. Once you settle down, stuff like this is just to think of around the fire. I got two kids, and Sarah's due to birth another one next month. This is my last shot at playin' ball with you guys. Let's do it right, kick some tail, and have fun!"

Junior pulled a pack of cards from his pocket. "Boo-ray,

anybody? Let's do somethin'!"

Rafe shook his head and stood. "Not me. I gotta get outa this room and get some air. Anybody wanta walk down the street and maybe see a movie?"

Blue Daddy, Willy B, and Jimmy Lee arose to accompany Rafe. Hump looked significantly at Buzz, then stood himself. "Reckon I'll go along to keep y'all outa trouble. We'll be back early."

"No beer," warned Buzz.

"No beer," agreed Rafe.

Junior draped a blanket across the foot of one of the beds and pulled up a chair to it. Buzz pulled his seat up, and Spider sat crosslegged on the floor. Caleb and Wilber waved "No thanks" and settled back to watch a television program. Buzz beckoned to Third.

"C'mon, Third. Can't play no three-handed boo-ray." The blonde nodded and pulled up another chair. Junior dealt as Buzz leaned over to pull a sock full of pennies from his suitcase. "Penny ante," the captain suggested, counting out a quarter's worth to all four. "You can pay the bank after we're through, or buy more pennies along, from the pot."

When the movie-goers returned, it was obvious that the Barefoot Dodger captain was on a streak. Coins and even a dollar bill were piled in front of Buzz, and a pot had built up that probably totaled another two dollars. Hump knelt behind Third. "Ole Buzz dealin' off the bottom?" he asked.

Spades were trumps, and Third had only one, a five. Junior broke trumps but was overtrumped by Buzz, who then played the ace and king of spades, obviously going for a run and trying to boo his tablemates. Spider, anticipating just that, began to count the pot. Hump noticed that Third had played void on both trump tricks. When Buzz led the ten of spades, it walked, and Third played void again, keeping his eyes downcast. Buzz triumphantly threw down his last card, an ace of diamonds. "Booed y'all! Three pot matches!" he crowed.

But Third played his trump and pulled the last trick to his side. "Whew! Thought I was gone," he sighed.

Buzz sat disappointed for a second, then reached to look at the last two tricks. "Hey, wait a minute! You played void, didn't you? I thought...."

Third smothered a laugh, then owned up as the captain began to get mad. "Hey, I was just jokin'! I knew you had us all booed right from the start. Here," he tossed the trick to Buzz.

"Wait! If Third hadn't reneged, I'da got one trick," protested Spider, reaching to flip over the cards.

"Naw, man, I'da taken one!" Junior claimed. "I ain't booin' that hand, Buzz. If Third hadn'ta reneged, my queen mighta walked when you played...."

"Aw right! Game's over! Nobody has to match! Nobody booed, okay?" Buzz was close to losing his temper, especially with the movie-goers back and laughing at him.

"Hey, wait. I'm sorry, Buzz. Here, I'll match for everybody, okay?" Third began to count out his coins.

Uncle Eb stuck his head in the door. "Lights out...you boys gamblin'? What'd I tell y'all about that? Bible says...."

"We was just messin' around, Uncle Eb, and had just broke up to go to bed," Buzz explained hastily. "Soon as everybody clears outa mine and Hump's room."

"Lotta folks in here, all right. Hit the hay, boys, y'all gotta big game tomorrow," the old man directed.

As Uncle Eb exited, Third stood and offered Buzz a hand. "I was just kiddin', Buzz. I'll make it up to you."

Buzz shook, scowling mock-fiercely. "Third, there's two kinds of people in this room: niggers and renegers! Keep your durned ole money and bet it on the Barefoot Dodgers tomorrow!"

The blonde grinned. "Niggers and renegers, huh? I'll go double or nothin' on you pitchin' a shutout tomorrow."

"I pitched today! What about a shutout through five innings?" his friend asked.

"You're on! Good luck and good night, you guys."

Hump asked as he turned off the light, "You feel good enough to throw a shutout after throwin' a game today? You ain't tight no more?"

"I'm loose. I feel good -- damn good!" Buzz grinned.

Chapter Fifteen

The Woodville Owls had won the losers bracket, and were set to play the Barefoot Dodgers Sunday afternoon for the state championship. Having already played three games, the Owls' pitchers were not sharp, and Willy B beat out a slow roller to third to open the game, stole second, and came in on Caleb's single to right. Hump advanced the runner on a hit and run play, and Buzz doubled into the gap in rightcenter for an RBI. The captain stole third when Jimmy Lee squared around to fake a bunt, then came home on a daring two-out, two-strike squeeze bunt.

With a three-run lead, Buzz took the mound and called his infielders in. "Looka here, guys, I feel good today! Let's show these dudes some classy baseball, okay? Junior, you loose? Jimmy Lee, let's just have some fun out here today! Spider, play like we're practicin' on Brownspur. Let's look good, everybody."

"What's got into you?" Blue Daddy asked. "Thought you was uptight about makin' a mistake; you high on somethin'?"

"I dunno," the pitcher mused. "I just...feel good. I just feel like can't nobody beat us today. You ever feel thataway?"

"Felt like that before Amazin' Gracie," Spider pointed out.

"And we kicked tail, didn't we? Let's just have some fun! Hump, I'm gonna try that palm ball today, and if I go to my cap bill when I lean in for the sign, look for that sidearm slider."

Hump shook his head. "Okay, but don't get mad at me if they tee off on that palm ball; I ain't gonna call it unless there's two strikes. And don't throw that sidearm curve with runners on, 'cause I never know where the hell it's goin'!" The catcher shook his head as he walked back to the plate. "Fun!"

But it settled down the team. Buzz offered up the palm ball, which was really a sailer changeup, to the leadoff, and the Owl was so far ahead of the pitch that he actually swung, jerked his bat back, and swung again after the ball was in Hump's mitt. The catcher argued tongue-in-cheek with the umpire that, since there were already two strikes on the batter, that the second hitter should have one strike already against him when he stepped to the plate. Longmile, who had not been in on the mound conference, advanced and loyally supported his catcher, quitting just before the ump got mad. He did insist on being shown in the rule book that there was no provision for a four-strike call. During the argument, Spider called the outfielders in to convey Buzz's message and explain the four-strike controversy. Finally the umpire called, "Play ball!"

The sidearm curve broke over the plate for a second strike, and true to his prediction, Hump could not glove it. It rolled to the backstop, while the Owl coach came out to protest the call of a strike on a pitch that went for a passed ball outside. "It just broke might near a foot, Coach!" the umpire declared.

Spider turned and caught a pop-up behind his back, winking at Junior. Jimmy Lee pulled the old hidden ball trick on a runner leading off first after a single in the second. Rafe hauled in a fly with a Willie Mays-type catch. Blue Daddy speared a liner and then chased the runner down himself instead of flipping to Jimmy Lee. Longmile muttered and scratched his head. "What's got into them boys?"

"They're sure havin' fun," Luke commented mildly.

Buzz lost his bet with Third when the cleanup blasted a palm ball over the centerfield fence with a man on in the fourth. "Don't throw that'un no more," Hump warned. The pitcher grinned and pointed to the scoreboard, where a two was going up against the Dodgers' seven. The Owls rallied briefly in the sixth, when Rafe took the mound in relief after Buzz had been touched for successive singles to load the bases. Rafe warmed up, then promptly picked off the man on first when the umpire called, "Play ball!" Grinning, Buzz walked the ball to his relief.

"Betcha can't do it again," he challenged.

"Betcha a buck I can."

Longmile frowned as Rafe walked the first hitter to face him on four pitches. Hump called time and went to the mound. "Man, you ain't got nothin' on them pitches! What's wrong?"

"Ole Buzz bet me I couldn't pick off two in a row. I'm gonna waste one walk and pick this guy off."

"You crazy?" the catcher frowned.

"Naw. Just havin' fun. Hide and watch me nail this dude."

And he did. As the runner led off, the first base coach warned, "Careful, Billy, this guy's got a good move." The runner glanced quickly to nod his understanding, just as Rafe whirled.

The Owl coach argued the call, but there was no doubt that Buzz's tag had been in time. The infielders met at the mound again while the discussion between coach and umpire was going on. Hump addressed Junior. "My turn now. Cover third when this guy leads off. This batter's a lefty, so I'm gonna have Rafe pitchout and peg it to you, okay?"

"Do it," Junior nodded.

It worked just as planned. For the first time in his long baseball career, Longmile had seen all three outs in an inning come from baserunners being picked off. "Ole Rafe's got a major league move," Uncle Eb observed.

"Hump's ain't bad either," the coach replied proudly.

Wilber again closed out the game, actually striking out a man in the ninth, something he never did. When Spider turned his back and made a running, spearing catch of a dying quail in shallow left for the final out, the Barefoot Dodgers charged the mound and carried Wilber from the field in triumph. Longmile and Buzz accepted the state championship trophy in a ceremony at home plate, and Bubba Duncan saw it on the six o'clock news back home.

"That's OUR boys! The Barefoot Dodgers!" he exclaimed to his wife. "State Champs!"

Chapter Sixteen

Mr. Leroy hosted the new champions at a barbeque back at Brownspur that evening. Actually, the celebration had been planned for Jackson, if there was to be one. However, with the Dodgers sweeping the tournament through the winner's bracket, it was decided that it might be best to make the two-hour drive before dark. A couple of phone calls assured that preparations would be made for the team's arrival, and Mr. Leroy packed the food back in his car. "This'll be well-traveled barbeque," he remarked to his wife, "but the charm of the Rally Pigs worked again!"

One of the calls had been to Bubba Duncan, who had local news coverage alerted, and there was quite a crowd at the victory party Mr. Wood had set up at the commissary that evening. None of the Dodgers had changed out of their uniforms, so both newspaper and television photographers and cameramen were happy, as were the boys. The excitement was too much for Wilber's wife, who had early labor pains and was rushed to the hospital for the night. While it was not quite her time, the doctor warned Wilber that the baby would probably come soon, but there did not seem to be any complications.

The party broke up soon after that, and most of the Barefoot Dodgers headed homeward. Some, however, were still in a celebrating mood. "Let's go to town for a couple of beers, y'all," Junior suggested.

"Suits me," Jimmy Lee agreed.

Rafe and Blue Daddy had other plans, however. "We gonna jam for awhile here at the shop," Blue declared. "Why don't y'all just bring us some back?"

"Thought y'all couldn't drink in here," Willy B observed.

"Can't. But, time these guys have a few brews and get back out here to Brownspur, we'll be ready to close up and kick back for awhile. Okay?" Rafe asked.

"Suits me," Jimmy Lee repeated. "Anybody else wanta go to town?" But there were no takers, Willy B and Spider deciding to stay and listen to the jam session. The rest had gone home. Jimmy Lee and Junior changed out of their uniforms and drove off in the former's Chevrolet.

It was two hours later when the music session wound down, and the pair who had gone for beer had still not returned. Rafe had cut out the lights and was locking the shop when the four heard the sound of an approaching vehicle.

"Man! They're comin' fast! Reckon that's Junior and Jimmy Lee?" Willy B asked anxiously.

"Hope not, but I bet it is," Blue answered. "Hey, all the lights are out now, better try to wave 'em down, or they'll think we're all gone home already." He walked to the side of the road as the approaching headlights neared, still dangerously fast.

"Hey, you guys," Spider yelled, standing at the front of the shop waving. The car shot by him, and then brake lights came on, as the driver obviously glimpsed movement at the darkened shop. The car swayed dangerously. "Hold it in the road!" Spider exclaimed, as if the driver could hear him.

"WHOOOAAAA!!!" Blue Daddy bellowed, but it was too late. The car veered right, jerked back left, then began to roll over. It hit the big post at the corner of the catchpen, bounced back upright, skidded into the pasture, and flipped over, coming to a stop on its side. "Junior!" yelled Blue Daddy, and sprinted toward the wreck with his comrades.

Jimmy Lee had been thrown clear, and was lying with his right leg twisted unnaturally, moaning. Junior was in the front seat, blood visible on his head, but moving. Spider kicked out the broken windshield and reached in. "Junior! You okay, man? Can you move everything? Get on out before it catches fire!"

"Help me get him out," Willy B had crawled into the car. "He's movin' his legs okay, so his back must be all right." The three boys dragged the injured one clear. His head was bloody and had a knot on it, but none of the cuts seemed deep. His left arm, however, was badly broken, a compound fracture. "Arm's busted, and so is Jimmy Lee's leg," Willy B proclaimed. "Y'all watch 'em while I run across the pasture to get Mr. Leroy."

Jimmy Lee regained consciousness in Rafe's arms. "Helluva party, huh?" he grimaced. "My car gonna be okay? What's wrong with my leg? Where's Junior?"

"He's got a busted arm and some cuts. How fast were y'all goin'?!" Spider wondered.

"Got her up to a hunnerd and ten!" the driver boasted. "Oh, we brought y'all some beer back. Damn, my leg hurts!"

"Believe I'll pass," Blue Daddy said sadly. "Looks like y'all two drunk enough beer for the whole damn team!"

TEAM _Barefoot Dodgers_   RECORD   TEAM   RE

NO.	PLAYERS	B/A	POS INN	1	2	3	4	5	6
1	Willy B	RF				1-3	F9		
	SUB. Brown Bro	RF	PH 6						
	SUB.								
2	Jimmy Lee	1B							
	SUB. Sherman	2B	4	E3	61	RBI			
	SUB.								
3	Buzz	P	1B 4			F7		F7	
	SUB. III	1B	6						
	SUB.								
4	HUMP	C			F8			E4	
	SUB.					RBI			RBI
	SUB.								
5	Caleb	LF		6-4				F8	
	SUB.								
	SUB.								
6	Spider	SS		6-4-3				6-3	
	SUB.						RBI		
	SUB.								
7	RAFE	CF	P 4		5-3	3-4			
	SUB. Hay-Sue	CF	4						
	SUB.								
8	Junior	3B		F9		4-3	4		
	SUB. Luke		PH 5						
	SUB. Red	3B	P 5						
9	Blue Daddy	2B	P 6		K				
	SUB. Wilbur	2B	P 6				2 RBI		
	SUB.								
	SUB.								
	SUB.								
	Coach - Longmile								
	SUB.								
	SUB.								
UMPIRE _Uncle Eb_				R 4 3	R 3 2	R 1 1	R 1 0	R	R
UMPIRE				LOB 1 / ER 1	LOB 2 / ER 1	LOB 1 / ER	LOB 1 / ER	LOB / ER	LOB
UMPIRE				E	E	E	E	E	E
SCORER				B/6		B/6			

Chapter Seventeen

Longmile tapped on the office door, catching Mr. Leroy just finishing up a phone conversation. The owner motioned him in and flipped the drink machine key at him, gesturing with two fingers. When the drinks returned, he was off the phone and held the pint bottle of clear liquid toward Longmile. "What's on your mind?"

It was apparent that the Negro was troubled. He considered the pint, then shook his head and handed it back. "Bossman, I need some help."

So addressed, the bossman declined the pint himself and stuck it back in the file. This was evidently serious business.

The coach sighed and began, "You know Junior and Jimmy Lee was hurt pretty bad in that wreck last night?"

"Yeah, but they'll be all right. A broke leg and a broke arm ain't bad for takin' out a corner of the catchpen fence and rollin' that Chevy halfway across the pasture. Doc said they'd both been drinkin' pretty heavy; celebratin' winnin' the State Championship, I guess?"

Longmile nodded sourly. "And me preachin' to them boys about goin' to bed early this week before we head to Birmingham. I got problems fieldin' a team now that we won the state. You know Wilber's wife's fixin' to foal again soon? He says he's through playin' for good. That's three players out in a day's time, and Doc says Sherman's ankle won't be out of a cast for another month. Serves him right, tryin' to break that new colt bareback! Mr. Leroy, you realize we ain't got enough black Barefoot Dodgers left to field a team?!"

His listener sat up in consternation, and began to tick off the healthy players on his fingers. "Let's see, Buzz pitchin', Hump catchin', Blue on second, Spider at short, and Caleb, Rafe, and Willy B in the outfield. Longmile, you're right! You ain't got enough. Can you get some substitutes?"

"Well, they'd have to be from the same locality and the right age -- and on the roster. See, I had to turn in a roster and birth dates when we entered the league. Anybody ain't on the roster can't play in the tournaments."

"So, you ain't got anybody else. Surely there's a hardship rule where they'll let some of the other players from nearby teams play with us. Hey, what if we could get that little third baseman from Goose Hollow? Bet he'd fill Junior's shoes. And there's a great first baseman with the DunDeal team, who even pitches left-handed. If we...."

"Nossir, we can't," Longmile interrupted firmly. "Gotta be roster players, period."

His boss was hopeless, "So, I guess the Woodville Owls, that we beat for the championship, will get to go to the regional playoffs? Dammit!" he swore. "I already had reservations for Birmingham, for the whole family. Reckon I'll just cancel."

"Weeelll...." Longmile hedged. "There's still a chance we could go, but I'd need you to talk to some of the boys to see if they'd play. If you don't mind."

"Hell naw! Who? I'll twist their arms, if I need to!"

"Weeelll...." the coach was clearly uneasy.

"Who, man?"

"Well, sir," the black took a deep breath, "it's Third, Red, and Hey-Sue. Reckon they'd mind playing with the Barefoot Dodgers officially?"

The owner was flabbergasted. "Who? What the hell are you talkin' about, Longmile?"

The coach leaned forward earnestly to make a full confession. "Can I have that drink now?" he asked first. Mutely, the pint was offered to him, and he went through the ritual of pouring some into his soft drink and shaking the bottle. He took a deep pull at the bottle, grimaced, and plunged right in: "Mr. Leroy. When I signed us up for the International Amateur League, they required a minimum of fifteen players on a team roster. I had eleven blacks the right ages that played ball, and that's all we ever needed. But since I had to list fifteen names, and your boys played with us all the time except for games, I listed Third, Luke, Red, and Hey-Sue. Hell, all I was doin' was followin' rules. I didn't mean no harm."

Mr. Leroy was dumbstruck. "But I thought it was a black league? You gonna paint my boy black? Dammit, make some sense, Longmile, before I take a bat to you!"

The Negro rolled his eyes apologetically and reached for his back pocket. "I'm sorry, Bossman. I never meant nothin' by it. Like I say, your boys grew up with mine, and they played together since they were knee-high to a junebug. But you know how all this race stuff is nowadays. Man can't tell what color he is before seein' the newspaper every day. Used to be, we was colored; now they say we ain't -- we're black. Used to be we was Nee-Grows," he purposely emphasized the sound, "but somebody objected to nigger, and that's a no-no. I grew up a darky, until somebody with more mouth than sense said that was bad. There's Afro-Americans, brothers, spooks, spades, and bluegums, just like there's white trash, rednecks, nabobs, peckerwoods, and hooproobins." He noticed his employer's eyebrows beginning to rise and held up his hand to forestall an interruption.

"What I mean is, Mr. Leroy, there's so many black folks objectin' to what label we's wearin' that day, that this set of league rules don't have nothin' I can find sayin' a team gotta have all blacks -- or any blacks, for that matter. You read it and see

The Barefoot Dodgers

if there's anything against a bunch of friends from Brownspur playin' baseball together in the International Amateur League!"

The owner accepted the papers in silence, and leaned back in his chair, pausing only to toss the drink machine key to the coach. When the drinks returned, the pint bottle was applied to both liberally, and Mr. Leroy drained half of his in one pull. He read the two-page set of league rules, jaw muscles working, then took one more swig before leaning his chair forward and placing his feet on the floor. He looked levelly at Longmile and spoke deliberately.

"You mean you want me to talk Third, Red, and Hey-Sue into playing baseball for a shot at a national championship, with a group of guys they've grown up with and play with nearly every day? I can tell you now that either of my sons would jump at the chance. But what about the rest of the Dodgers? Will they let 'em play? I don't want anyone gettin' hurt here. What about the other teams? Will this make bad blood?"

"You think they'd play, sho'nuff?"

"Hell, I know they would! Luke's been on the bench right beside you nearly every game, and Third's been there when his own American Legion team wasn't playing. But what about your guys? Will they think they'll get labeled as Uncle Toms? The Brownspur Uncle Toms -- now, that's a name for you!"

Longmile now saw that his chances were good, and waxed more enthusiastic. "Uncle Toms? Trouble? Who was the first kid to hit that big ole center fielder from the Trilakes Growlin' Cubs when he took out Hump at the plate that time? Li'l ole Red-Headed PeckerWood! And right behind him was Third! They come off the fence and was in the pile before Buzz could get there from the mound. Red'll jump right up in anybody's face, but race don't make no never mind with him; he's just hot-headed. Only black boy might give us trouble is Willy B, raggin' Hey-Sue.

The Barefoot Dodgers

He don't cut that Mexican boy no slack, but so far Hey-Sue is just takin' it. One-a these days, them two are gonna tangle, and that'll be good for everybody. But you know yourself that the white boys ain't really accepted Hey-Sue either." He paused for breath. "Mr. Leroy, folks up north think we don't get along down south. I betcha these kids from Brownspur could not only play a helluva baseball game, but show the whole world how blacks and whites ought to be friends. Hell," he declared bitterly, "at their age is when it's easy to get along. Even these boys'll get over it in another five years or so. But now...?"

Mr. Leroy dropped his head and looked at the floor for a moment. Then he swiveled and stared at the wall. When his shoulders started shaking, Longmile was mystified; then he heard the chuckles.

The plantation owner spun around and slammed his fist onto the desk, caught the overturning pint bottle, and pitched it to his coach, then broke out in peals of laughter. Longmile poured the rest of the pint into the two drink bottles, his own face beginning to twitch. Then he could hold it no longer: breaking into a huge grin, he asked, "You'll go along with it?"

The white man slapped his knee, roaring, "Damn straight! And Longmile -- we're gonna kick tail and take names!" He paused to catch his breath, and lifted his bottle in a toast: "To the Barefoot Dodgers! Best baseball team in the..." he glanced at the league papers, "...International Amateur League!" They touched glasses.

"Thank you, Sir!" the coach exclaimed.

His employer gripped him by the shoulder. "No, Longmile, thank you -- from a daddy!" Then he sobered. "But promise me one thing -- you'll take care of my boys. Every damn one of them, whatever color they are!"

TEAM *Barefoot Dodgers* RECORD TEAM R

NO.	PLAYERS	B/A	POS INN	1	2	3	4	5	6
1	Willy B	RF				1-3	F9		
	SUB. Brown Bro	Rf	P½						
2	Jimmy Lee	1B							
	SUB. Sherman	2B	4	E30	61	RBI			
3	Buzz	P	1B 4			F7		F7	
	SUB. II	1B	6						
4	Hump	C			F8		E4		
	SUB.				RBI		RBI		
5	Caleb	LF		6-4			F8		
	SUB.								
6	Spider	SS		1-4-3	1-0	6-3			
	SUB.					RBI			
7	Rafe	CF P4			5-3	3-4			
	SUB. Hay-Sue	CF	4						
8	Junior	3B		F9	4-3	4			
	SUB. Luke		BN/5						
	SUB. Red	3B	P4/5						
9	Blue Daddy	2B			4				
	SUB. Wilbur 6th	2B	P6			2 RBI			
	SUB.								
	SUB.								
	SUB.								
Coach - Longmile									
	SUB.								
	SUB.								
UMPIRE *Uncle Eb*				4 3	R3 2	R 1	R 0	R	R
UMPIRE				LOB / ER	LOB 2	LOB / ER	LOB / ER	LOB ER	LOB ER
UMPIRE				E	E	E	E	E	E
SCORER				D/P		D/P			

100   *The Barefoot Dodgers*

Chapter Eighteen

"Excuse me?" Third Alexander said to his father. "You want me to play in a real game with the Barefoot Dodgers? With the darkies? Now, how in the heck is that gonna work? White boys playin' in a black league!"

Luke's reaction was slightly different: "Hey, I'm on the roster too?! Great! Reckon they'll let me pinch hit? 'Luke's homer wins it in the bottom of the ninth!' What a headline! Shoot, yeah, we'll play!"

Third hedged, "Wait a minute, Luke. We're white."

Their father explained, "But the official league rules don't say anything atall about race. It's just that the only teams they approached were black teams at the time. Longmile had to list fifteen players on his roster, so he listed y'all too, never dreamin' he'd get four guys out and need y'all. Personally, I think it's a helluva opportunity, but I'll leave it up to you."

Luke glanced sideways at his brother. "Longmile's already told me I can be on the bench keepin' score like I always do. But I know it ain't me they want to play; it's you. If I was to get in, I know it'd just be a fluke -- maybe a pinch hit where I could swing for the fences and not have to run. But they really need you, Third. And Red'll play if you will."

"Hey, don't get me wrong," Third admonished, "I'd get a kick out of playin'. But what'll all the other teams say? Daddy, you think we'd stand a chance of gettin' hurt?"

Mr. Leroy frowned and shook his head. "Longmile and I talked that out. He's puttin' it up to the rest of the team today, and that's gonna be part of the package: anybody hassles y'all, the whole team goes after 'em. And, if any of the other Dodgers have their doubts about this, they'll have to talk it out now. If you go to the regionals, you go as a team, not as whites and blacks on a team. I've already talked to Buzz, since he's the captain, and he's all for it. If anybody can sell it, Buzz can. This could be a big chance for him, especially. There'll be pro scouts galore at the tournaments, both regional and national."

Luke chimed back in. "And you'd give us an extra pitcher, too, Third." Neither of his audience missed the "us."

The towhead grinned, "Hey, I'm in. You ain't got to twist my arm. But only if all the team is comfortable playin' with white boys. I think it'd be fun, but then we've been brought up playin' with these guys. Blacks from other places might take some shots at us, especially Red. Be some cleats flashin' on plays at third base, I bet."

His father countered, "Yeah, but if anyone can take care of himself, it'd be Red. He gets in fights with no regard for race, color, or creed, as the sayin' goes." He surveyed his sons. "So, y'all are for it? You'll play?"

Luke nodded enthusiastically, and Third gave a thumb's up motion. But he added, "As long as the rest of the Barefoot Dodgers are for us goin'. If even Willy B's against it, I don't think it'd be a good idea." He paused. "And I'll get Red, too. He was plannin' on goin' to the regionals with us anyway. You are still goin', aren't you, Daddy?"

"Heck, yeah! I already had reservations for rooms for y'all and your momma an' me. Red's folks had said he could go and room with y'all. Way Longmile and I have it figured out, I'll be able to sit in the dugout as team owner, and that way I can be close to the action if anything starts gettin' outa line. Each team also has to provide an umpire, so Uncle Eb will be along, too. That'll make three adults with the team, one of whom will have the power to throw an opposin' player out of the game if he gets to playin' rough. Or coach either. Longmile had talked it over with

Uncle Eb before he came to me, and he said it was God's will that y'all be the first white boys to integrate this Negro baseball league." He chuckled, and the boys joined him. "That's a helluva note: white boys from Mississippi integratin' somethin' that's been all black up to now. You two will be famous!"

"Yessir. But will the hullabaloo keep us from winnin'?" Third wondered.

"That's gonna be up to you, partly," Luke noted. "I've seen the tournament schedule, and we'll be playin' maybe six games in four days. If the Dodgers had to go with just two pitchers -- Rafe and Buzz -- it'd be tough. With you as a third pitcher, we'll stand a whole lot better chance. Wilber's havin' a baby, so he ain't goin', but he wasn't real good anyway. You might be the difference in the Barefoot Dodgers goin' to the nationals, Third. When you're on, you're good. And when you've got that sidearm curve breakin' sharp, ain't anybody in any league can get it outa the infield on you," he observed loyally.

His brother grinned cockily, "Hey, I'll mow 'em down; you just concentrate on gettin' me that one run in the bottom of the ninth, Hero!"

Their team owner clapped them both on the shoulders. "Just remember: 'Pride goeth before a fall.' Take 'em one at a time. And Third," he turned serious, "If y'all do play in this thing, better put a lid on bein' cocky or flashy."

"No sweat," his son assured him. "If we play."

TEAM *Barefoot Dodgers*   RECORD   TEAM   R

NO.	PLAYERS	B/A	POS INN	1	2	3	4	5	6
1	Willy B	RF				1-3	F9		
	SUB. Brown Bro	RF PH							
	SUB.								
2	Jimmy Lee	1B							
	SUB. Sherman	2B 4		E3	61	RBI			
	SUB.								
3	Buzz	P 1B 4				F9		F7	
	SUB. III	1B 6							
	SUB.								
4	HUMP	C		F8			E4		
	SUB.			RBI			RBI		
	SUB.								
5	Caleb	LF		6-4			F8		
	SUB.								
	SUB.								
6	Spider	SS		6-4-3			6-3		
	SUB.				RBI				
	SUB.								
7	RAFE	CF P4		5-3	3-4				
	SUB. Hay-Sue	CF 4							
	SUB.								
8	Junior	3B		F9	4-3	K			
	SUB. Luke	PH 5							
	SUB. Red	3B P 5							
9	Blue Daddy	2B		K					
	SUB. Wilbur 4th	2B P6			2 RBI				
	SUB.								
	SUB.								
	SUB.								
Coach-Longmile									
	SUB.								
	SUB.								
UMPIRE Uncle Eb				R 4	R 3	R 1	R 1	R 0	R
UMPIRE				LOB 1 / ER 1	LOB 2 / ER	LOB 1 / ER 1	LOB / ER	LOB
UMPIRE				E	E	E	E	E
SCORER				B/p		B/p			

Chapter Nineteen

"Say what?!!" Willy B Davidson exclaimed.

"Can't no white boys play in this league!" Rafe declared.

"Man, you outa your gourd!" Spider Webb observed. "Them yankee niggers ain't gonna let no white boys play with us!"

Buzz Waterman shrugged. "Either they play, and we all watch out for 'em, or else none of us play. With Jimmy Lee and Junior in casts, Sherman playin' cowboy, and Wilber playin' pappy, ain't enough for us to field a team. I got no problem with 'em. We grew up playin' with Third and Red; heck, they was practicin' with us day before yesterday -- Third struck you out three times, Spider. Luke's been on the bench near'bout every game we've played. Hey-Sue is closer to my color than you are, Brown Brother. I say, let's just play baseball and show these city dudes how to get along." He paused, jaw working. "And I need this tournament, win or lose. There's gonna be scouts from every major league team watchin' and this might be a shot at the majors for me -- and some of you, too." He nodded toward Spider, Hump, and Rafe. "If it takes bein' the only team with white boys, well, I'll strap that on, and lay into anybody who looks sideways at one of our teammates!"

Hump, of course, had already discussed it with his father. Head jutted forward belligerently, he reminded Willy B, "Who was the first man to jump that Trilakes guy tried to knock me loose from the ball that time? Red! You's safe out there in right, but Red and Third come off the fence and balled the jack on that guy's gizzard! Shoot, I'll play with them two any day of the week, anywhere!"

Like Hump, Caleb had been informed of the scheme by his father the night before, and Uncle Eb had left no doubt as to which way he expected his boy to go. Speaking slowly as usual, the left fielder supported his captain and catcher. "I got no problem with it. I just wanta play baseball."

Blue Daddy had not lived on the plantation but a year, so he was a relative stranger to the system. Longmile picked him as the key to the matter. "What about you, Blue? You been to Atlanta and some cities. You reckon it'd cause too much of a ruckus to have white boys on the team?"

As usual, Blue struck up a rhythm on the bench with his fingernails to accompany his thoughts. "Well, sir," he tapped, "I get along plumb fine with all of 'em; even Hey-Sue. Lotta spics where I come from. And I been to see the Braves play a lot. Y'all seen 'em on teevee. White boys all over the field on every major league team, and the minors too. We played together in high school, and all colleges got blacks and whites playin' together. Way I see it, we ain't got a chance without 'em, for sure. With 'em...well, we all know Red's a better third baseman than Junior ever thought about bein'," he grimaced at having to say that about his own brother, "and Third gives us pitchin' depth. Hey-Sue ain't particularly good, but he'll give it a shot. We just gotta decide are we gonna back 'em up all the way with the other teams, 'cause they're sure gonna come after 'em!"

Longmile prodded, "And you're behind 'em? Or not?"

Blue Daddy grabbed a bat and with the little end of it, played a passable drum roll on the bench. "Hey, let's play ball!"

Uncle Eb stood and spit tobacco juice, wiping his chin with the back of his hand before he spoke. "One thing about it: if I'm callin' the game and anybody takes a shot at one of our guys, white or black, he's gone. Ain't gonna be no cussin' when I'm umpirin', either. Y'all know how I feel about that. So when I meet with these other teams, I'm gonna lay the law down. I can't help it if somebody's got rabbit ears, but I can keep the mean stuff down." He paused for effect, and spit again. "And that goes for both teams on the field, includin' y'all."

"We got to eat and shower with white boys?" Willy B wanted to know.

Buzz looked at him strangely. "You been swimmin' in the creek with 'em half the summer, and every other summer of your life, fool! And Mr. Leroy buys us all sody pops after practice and games. Damn, you sat there Saturday and ate sardines and viennies off the same knife with Red, and Luke was doin' the same thing with Hump! Whatcha mean, we gotta eat with 'em?"

The subject of his scorn had nearly as hot a temper as Red Wood, and replied in kind, "Well, that was out here, where we's friends and all. I mean we gotta eat with 'em in restaurants and suchlike in towns? And showerin' in a locker room is different than a swimmin' hole."

Uncle Eb reproved Buzz before answering, "Ain't no call for cussin', Buzz. Willy B, I ain't never noticed you backin' offa eatin' when anybody's around. But if showerin' with white boys bothers you, we'll chose up who goes first by who stinks the worst after the game. That way, you'll get through before anybody else on the team!" The old man grinned to remove any sting from his words.

Longmile stood to address his charges. "Well, here's the way I see it: we either go with white boys, or we don't go atall, 'cause we ain't got enough healthy niggers to field a team and the rules are you got to play nine men -- not eight, or ten. Ain't nobody else on our roster except Luke, Red, Third, and Hey-Sue, and we have to play roster players. We got two choices: play ball and try to whip them city niggers, or don't play ball. Which way y'all want to go?"

"Play!" declared Buzz, and raised his hand. Hump, Caleb,

Blue Daddy, and Spider quickly stuck hands in the air, along with Brown Brother. "You can't vote," Buzz told him, "you ain't old enough."

"I'm the batboy, and Luke's my best friend," replied the youngster. "I'll take a bat to anybody tries to mess with him!"

"He's a poet and don't know it!" teased Blue, and laughter broke the tension.

"How 'bout it, you two?" Longmile asked of Rafe and Willy B, the only ones not committed.

"Rafe's just scared Third'll roll him for his job," Hump jeered with a smile. "C'mon, y'all. Play or stay home."

"I'm in," Rafe shrugged. "If Third pitches too, it'll give us enough to maybe win. Ain't no way me and Buzz could throw six games in four days, especially with Wilber gone. And if I can get my fastball workin' while them pro scouts are watchin'-- well, I'll buy alla y'all Cadillacs with my signin' bonus!" He punched Willy B in the ribs. "C'mon, hardhead! Heck, you can use my soap; it's black, so you won't hafta worry about none of that white skin rubbin' off on you!"

Buzz reached his hand out to the lone holdout. "C'mon, man. We got this far together. We'll kick some tail and show them city folks how to play ball!"

Willy B sighed and shook hands with the captain. "Okay. I don't mind playin' with Red and Third. But y'all keep Hey-Sue outa my way. I ain't partial to no spic."

"Ooo-wee, man! You prejudiced!" Blue Daddy held his nose.

"Hey," Willy B rejoined, "you ain't seen prejudiced yet! You wait until we trot out on that field with a couple of white boys -- that's when you gonna see why I ain't charged up about this. Mark my words, we gonna hafta fight for our whites."

"You ain't got to if you don't want to," Hump growled. "I'll do the fightin'."

To everyone's surprise, it was Uncle Eb who stepped forward to correct him. "Nawp, if anybody tangles, it better be every Barefoot Dodger in the pile. 'Cause we ain't got enough players for me to throw even one outa the game. Rules say you can't throw the whole team out -- just the ones who start it. Not countin' Luke, we got one extra man. Gotta be all for one and one for all, just like in the Bible!"

There was a moment of silence while the team digested his edict. Then Spider frowned. "Whereabouts is that in the Bible?"

The old umpire shook his head sorrowfully. "Ain't I just been wastin' my time tryin' to teach y'all Sunday School all these years!? That's your assignment for Sunday, Spider. You better gimme chapter and verse on it, or you gotta clean out the ladies' rest room Sunday afternoon."

"Awww, maaann...."

Brown Brother punched the shortstop in the ribs and whispered, "Hey, just ask Luke. He knows the Bible backards and forwards."

"Everybody out!" Longmile ordered. "We gotta practice. Look out, Birmingham!"

NO.	PLAYERS	B/A	POS INN	1	2	3	4	5	6
1	Willy B	RF		◇ ①	◇	⌐3	⌐9		
	SUB. Brown Boo	RF	P4 6						
	SUB.								
2	Jimmy Lee	1B		◇	◇			◇	
	SUB. Sherman	2B	4	E3	E1	RBI			
	SUB.								
3	Buzz	P 1B 4		◇	◇	⌐7		⌐7	
	SUB. III	1B	6						
	SUB.								
4	HUMP	C		◇	⌐8		◇	E6	
	SUB.					RBI			RBI
	SUB.								
5	CALEB	LF		6-4			◇	⌐8	
	SUB.								
	SUB.								
6	SPider	SS		6·4·3			◇	6-3	
	SUB.						RBI		
	SUB.								
7	RAFE	CF P4		◇	5-3		3-4		
	SUB. HAY-Sue	CF	4						
	SUB.								
8	Junior	3B		⌐9		4-3	4		
	SUB. Luke		PH5						
	SUB. Red	3B	P6						
9	Blue Paddy	2B		K	◇				
	SUB. Wilbur 4th	2B	P6		O				
	SUB.				2 RBI				
	SUB.								
	SUB.								
	Coach - Longmile								
	SUB.								
	SUB.								
UMPIRE	Uncle Eb			R 4 3 LOB 1 ER 1	R 3 2 LOB 3 ER 1	R 1 1 LOB 1 OER	R 1 0 LOB 1 ER	R LOB ER	R LOB
UMPIRE									
UMPIRE			E	E	E	E	E	E
SCORER			B/p		B/p			

Chapter Twenty

It was a total surprise to officials of the International Amateur League when the Mississippi champions took the field to warm up with three white boys and a Mexican in uniform. One of the whites fungoed flies to the outfield, while two others played the corners of the infield. Several of the fly balls went over the fence in deep center before the kid hitting them apparently got the range and eased off on his power. Their opponents sat wonderingly in the dugout, awaiting their turn in the field, and anticipating that the joke would soon be revealed unto them. Longmile and Uncle Eb approached the pressbox. Mr. Leroy had wisely decreed that they should fight the fight themselves.

The tournament chairman was also the Southern rep for the IAL, and Birmingham was his home town. While his team had not made the finals in Alabama, he was a moderately successful small college coach, who had turned out some major leaguers in his time. "What's the deal with these white boys, Coach?" he asked, hoping that the Caucasians were just helping the Barefoot Dodgers warm up.

"Well, I got three of 'em on my approved roster, plus the Mexican boy. I figure to kick some tail with my white boys."

"You can't play no white boys in this tournament."

"Show me in the rules where it says that," was Longmile's rejoinder. He pulled out the paperwork in question and slapped it on the table. "Show me," he dared.

The chairman went directly to the paragraph where he expected to find the needed information, and stammered, "But... but...but even if it don't say it, everybody knows...."

"It's gotta say it in writing," Longmile stated firmly. "Look, you know and I know this is supposed to be a black league, but it don't say it in the rules nowhere. I never figured on usin' 'em, but I lost four players in the past few weeks, and I had put these kids what practiced with us regular on the roster so I'd have fifteen. Then I found out there wasn't no rule against white boys playin' even though I knew it was supposed to be one of them unwritten rules -- like blacks goin' to the back of the bus?" he jabbed.

"Hey, man, I don't write the rules, I just enforce them."

"Exactly!" Uncle Eb agreed. "There ain't no rule against white boys playin', so just enforce that with these other teams."

"But...but...I gotta call IAL headquarters."

Longmile laughed, "He sounds like my old fishin' motor: 'but, but, but, but, but.' Just make it quick, Coach. 'Cause we got a game here in twenty minutes. And my white boys are gonna play!"

Just then the coach of the opposing team strolled into the room. He was a tall, easy-going man whose teams Longmile had competed with for years. "What's goin' on, Longmile? I see you gotta play your bossman's sons? That the only way you could get him to buy uniforms?"

"Hey, Rufus," the short coach greeted the tall one. Actually, Longmile knew that this was the one team he'd have no trouble out of, for the Arkansas champions were also a plantation team, the only other one in the playoffs. If any other coach would support him, it would be Rufus Calcote. The white owner of the team had even accompanied the Desha County Dusters, as Mr. Leroy had the Brownspur Barefoot Dodgers.

"Looka here, Rufe," he began, "I had some bad luck this past month. One of my outfielders broke an ankle breakin' a bronco, and my relief pitcher's havin' a baby this week. Or rather, his wife is," he corrected himself. "Then the Saturday night after we won the state championship, my first baseman and third baseman celebrated too much and rolled their car. Broke an arm and a leg.

If it weren't for bad luck...." Longmile shook his head.

"So, you really do gotta play them white boys, doncha?"

"Sho'nuff. I had eleven blacks, and to make out my fifteen-man roster I put down the other kids had been practicin' with us. Never dreamed I'd have to play 'em. But you know the rules: we can't play non-roster players."

Rufus frowned. "Don't the rules also say 'black' somewhere?"

"Not atall. I searched and searched, but there ain't nowhere in there it says only blacks can play. 'Course," Longmile winked smilingly, "You and me was brought up cotton patch niggers, then got to be colored, then Nee-grows, and for a while, I'da fought someone for callin' me black. Funny world, ain't it?"

The Arkansas coach chuckled, "I know what you mean. But I can't believe there ain't nothin' in the rules about playin' whites."

"There ain't!" interposed the tournament chairman from the door. "I just called headquarters and talked to a lawyer, and he says the same thing. Longmile, there ain't nothin' to keep you from playin' them white boys, but I can't condone it atall. It ain't in the spirit of things, and you'll just make trouble! I gotta ask you to withdraw your team."

"Ain't no way!" was the response. "And there ain't no way you can make me!"

"What's the problem?" Rufus Calcote shrugged. "My team's been practicin' with white boys, and played two games with a white catcher when my catcher had the mumps and they went down on him. Here's my lineup, Ump," he handed a sheet to Uncle Eb, who had been surprisingly quiet during the exchange. "Coach, if y'all are through warmin' up, we'll take the field." He paused at the door to grin back, "And kick your lily-white tails!"

"In your dreams!" roared Longmile.

The tournament director threw up his hands.

"Let's play ball," declared Uncle Eb, following Longmile out the door.

Chapter Twenty-One

It had been one helluva tournament, Longmile thought with satisfaction as the school bus rumbled through the night on the four-hour drive home. It had been good to loosen up on the Arkansas team, which had been beaten twice during the season by the Barefoot Dodgers. Most of the kids knew each other, and there had been no animosity to interfere with baseball. Other than a close play at second, when Red Wood had taken out the shortstop -- but cleanly -- to prevent Caleb's being doubled up, there had been little fuss in that first game. Buzz had pitched seven good innings, Hump had homered with two men on in the third, and Rafe had come in to close out a shutout for Buzz. There had been some catcalls from the stands in regard to the whites playing with the Dodgers, but it had bothered no one. Luke had found a bar of licorice soap which he presented to Willy B after the game, with appropriate laughter from the team. And it really had been a team effort the rest of the way.

Rafe had started the second game, and was as on as his coach had ever seen him. The Georgia team got two hits, both scratch. One was a pooter topped to Red in the fourth by the lightning fast leadoff hitter, but Rafe had promptly picked him off first. If Rafe ever made it to the majors, Longmile mused, it would be his pickoff move that would make the difference. Rafe had tired a little in the eighth, and had given up a leadoff double off the wall in right. Bringing Third in from first to pitch, pulling Buzz to first from center, and sending Hey-Sue to centerfield had been Longmile's moves. The towheaded southpaw junkballer, coming in behind the fireballing righty, completely befuddled the Georgians, and Third only threw nine pitches to close out the game, four of them pop-ups to Red. Rafe had been just as formidible with the bat, too, going three for four and scoring twice, with an RBI himself. The Dodgers won eight to zip, and carried Rafe from the field, Buzz under one hip, and Third under the other.

A trifle fearfully, Longmile had started Third against the Tennessee team in the third game. While he had confidence in Third's ability, he was unsure whether the youngster would be able to handle the spotlight under the circumstances. His intuitions were correct, for Third's heart was in his throat as never before, though he would have died before admitting it. Their fears were all for naught, however, for the Volunteer State Pumas, like most of the teams, only had two good pitchers, and coming through the loser's bracket, they had already played three games before meeting the Barefoot Dodgers. Willy B led off the game with a single, Spider laced a double down the third base line, Caleb was intentionally walked to load the bases and set up a force play, then Hump cleaned up with a powerful blow into the left-field seats. The Dodgers batted around two of the first three innings and the game was called by the ten-run rule after five innings. Longmile was even able to pinchhit Luke for Blue Daddy in the fourth, and the CF Kid delivered a shot over the center field fence on the first pitch to him. Uncle Eb smilingly allowed Luke to take his time on the bases, and it was a barely winded, totally happy kid who crossed home plate to be carried by all his teammates to the dugout, where Mr. Leroy tearfully handed him an oxygen inhaler. Hey-Sue took Blue's place at second, and turned a nifty double play to Spider to end the game. Third gave up ten hits, but clearly was over his nervousness after three innings, and won eighteen to six.

The fourth game was the toughest, against a scrappy team from Lousiana. Their plan was hit, run, and steal, and Hump was so exhausted by the end of the game that Longmile was considering catching Willy B. But he had thrown out seven runners, and blocked the plate on a suicide squeeze when Third caught the movement from the corner of his eye and quickpitched sidearm. That saved the game in the bottom of the ninth, and in the eleventh, Red Wood caught the third baseman playing back and bunted safely, taking second on a throw in the dirt. Blue sacrificed him to third, and with the fielders drawn in, Willy B poked a fast ball over third to a charging left fielder who made a perfect throw home, but to no avail. Red wasn't big, but he was all heart and muscle, and the Colored Coonie's catcher never stood a chance. After the collision, the ball rolled free, Uncle Eb signaled "Safe!" and the benches emptied. Mr. Leroy grabbed Luke and Brown Brother, but other than that, the rest joined the fray. This was the semifinal game, and television cameras were present. That night on the news, Wilber, in Sarah's hospital room where she nursed their newborn son, saw Uncle Eb with a neckhold on Buzz, pulling him off a Coonie who was pulling Third off of the catcher, who had a grip on Red, who was trying to pummel the opposing pitcher, who was hammering Willy B, who was being held by the Colored Coonie coach, who was himself being pounded by Longmile. The IAL Southern Regionals Championship game had been between the Arkansas Dusters, coming up through the loser's bracket, and the Barefoot Dodgers. Longmile had used all three pitchers in the extra-inning game, and on a hunch started Rafe again. He walked four batters straight before finding the plate, but was then almost untouchable for five innings, when he lost it again. As before, Longmile brought his junkball, sidearming southpaw in to relieve the wild righty, and Third again set down the whole Arkansas order in three innings without a ball going out of the infield. Spider stretched a double into a triple in the third, and Caleb brought him home, then Buzz walked in the fifth, stole second, and came around on Third's bloop double on the line in right. Coach Rufus argued with the Ump's call on the play, but fortunately it wasn't Uncle Eb, who was calling third that day. Rufus was finally ejected, and Red Wood bounced the first pitch from a rattled Duster back through the box, bringing Third around with an insurance run, which he needed, for he relaxed and hung a curve to start the ninth. After the homer, Longmile brought Buzz in for the save, and he struck out the side on a dozen pitches, most of them knuckleballs.

The coach grinned and popped his own knuckles against the bus steering wheel. The Barefoot Dodgers, IAL Southern Champs, were headed to St Louis for the World Series of Amateur Baseball!

His third baseman noticed the grin and leaned forward, squinting from a blackened eye. "Hey, we're gonna show them yankees some real baseball, right, Coach?!"

Chapter Twenty-Two

It was two days later when Mr. Leroy Alexander got the phone call from the Alabama Highway Patrol.

"Mr. Alexander? This is Hiram Witherspoon, Chief of the Alabama Highway Patrol. You got time for me to ask you a couple of questions, sir?"

"Longmile musta been hustlin' back too fast," the farmer thought. Aloud, he replied, "Yessir, Chief. What's the problem?"

"Well, sir, we had a report that you signed the rental agreement on school bus number 13, from the Lee's Landing Consolidated School System, for a baseball team trip last week. Is that right, sir?"

"That's correct. Was Longmile goin' too fast on the way back home, Chief? We won, so maybe you could cut him some slack?" Mr. Leroy asked.

The Alabama officer replied negatively. "No, sir, he wasn't speedin' atall. We got an indecent exposure complaint against y'all, Mr. Alexander."

"A WHAT!!???"

"Yessir," the answer was matter of fact. "There was a lawyer and his wife comin' back from Tuscaloosa to Reform, and followin' your boys' bus for a spell. They claim that they got, well...mooned! From the back windows. I don't reckon you'd know anything about it?"

"MOONED!" Mr. Leroy screeched. "Is this a joke? Did Bubba Duncan put you up to this?"

"Mr. Alexander, I can assure you that this is no joke. I called you out of courtesy once I found out the circumstances. I admire your ball team's guts for playin' in that black tournament with white boys on the team," the voice drawled. "Said a couple of them were your sons? That right?"

The farmer got his temper under control. "That's so, Chief. Listen, I appreciate your courtesy. What can I do to keep this from gettin' outa hand? You know how boys are...."

The Chief chuckled. "Hey, I was young once, Mr. Alexander, and played on a championship baseball team, too. I can appreciate high spirits, especially from the winners. Here's what I believe would work: If you were to call and apologize to the couple what got mooned, and maybe get the boys that done it to either call or write a letter, I think I could get everything calmed down over thisaway. He was pretty hot under the collar to begin with, but when he found out it was a championship team, and I talked to him for a while, he backed off. Right now, no formal charges have been filed."

Mr.Leroy nodded. "I can do that, and I'll get the coach to talk to them, too. I wasn't on the bus; my wife and I spent an extra night with friends in Birmingham. Chief, I appreciate you bein' so understandin' about this. Now I just got to find out which one of them boys was moonin'...."

"One? That was what I thought was so fittin' and funny about this whole deal, Mr. Alexander," the officer laughed. "It wasn't just one."

The farmer hesitated. "Not just one? How do they know? With all due respect, it was night and I bet that bus was goin' sixty miles an hour over those hills and around those curves in west Alabama. Even if that guy is a lawyer, how's he gonna tell one black butt from another under those conditions?"

The laughter from the other end of the line was uproarious. "Because, Mr. Alexander, this was an equal-opportunity, fully integrated, non-discriminatory moonin', in black and white!"

There was a moment of silence before Mr. Leroy spoke

again, in a voice that reminded the Chief of ground glass. "Could you give me that lawyer's name, address, and phone number, Chief? I do believe that I can take care of this matter very well.... Thank you for callin', sir. I'm much obliged."

Hanging up the telephone, Mr. Leroy stormed to the front porch of the commissary. "THIRD! LUKE!" he bellowed across the pasture. "Get in here, NOW!"

"Now what?" asked Luke of his older brother. They had been engaged in mowing their back yard, but had heard their father's shout over the roar of the motors. Luke shut off the riding mower as Third throttled down the push mower he had been trimming close to the trees with.

The towhead shrugged into his tee shirt and beckoned. "I dunno, but we better hustle. There he goes again."

"THIRD! LUKE!" sounded across the plantation.

"COMIN'!" Third bellowed back. He held the fence strand up for Luke and the two fell into stride to cross the pasture. The CF Kid skipped a rock off of the stock pond surface.

Their father was standing on the porch waiting, red-faced. "What the HELL do you boys mean, embarrassin' me like that! I oughta tan your hides!" Mr. Leroy's finger shook in the boys' faces. "Dammit, I shoulda just let 'em arrest you!"

In all innocence, the brothers frowned up at their accuser. "We ain't done anything, Daddy! What...."

"MOONIN'!" Their parent was livid. "And not only that, but moonin' a lawyer! The Alabama Highway Patrol has a warrant out for y'all's arrest -- the arrest of the whole damn team! Y'all are gonna have to forfeit the tournament and...."

"NO! Not forfeit! We ain't gonna...." Third interrupted.

"SHUT UP! Who else was in on this?" Mr. Leroy exclaimed.

"On what?" Luke demanded. "What're y'all...."

"AHA!" the man pounced on his older son. "So it was you, Third! What the hell were you thinkin'? And who else was in on this joke? There was black and white bottoms involved."

"What joke?" Luke repeated. "Tell me what y'all are talkin' about, please, sir."

"I never said I was...." Third protested.

"You ain't got to say it," his father was grim. "You were the one knew what I was talkin' about. Now, who else was shinin' their butt out the back window?"

"I gotta tell?"

"What! Shinin' their...you mean somebody was moonin' outa the bus?" Luke clapped his hand over his mouth in horror. "I can't believe it!"

He got a dirty look from his sibling.

Mr. Leroy glared dangerously. "Damn right you got to tell me, and right now! Who?"

"Daddy, look. Lemme go talk to the team this afternoon. I'll get the other guy to come confess, okay?" Third pleaded.

His father considered. "Please don't be too hard on Third, Daddy. After all, we won the tournament," Luke added. Finally their parent nodded.

"Okay! But tonight, you both got to call and apologize to that lawyer and his wife. Understand? And I'm gonna be standin' over y'all listenin' to every damn word." He turned and stamped back through the commissary to his office, and slammed the door. He walked straight to the window and watched until he saw his sons walking back home across the pasture. Then he sat down in his swivel chair. And began to laugh. He laughed until he cried, as a matter of fact.

Third kicked savagely at a dried cow pie. "Dammit! How were we to know that guy behind us was a lawyer?"

Luke began to chuckle. "Looks like he'da dimmed his lights,

if he was a lawyer. How come you didn't play dumb, Third?"

His brother glanced sideways in annoyance, "Aw, he trapped me with that crack about forfeitin' the ball games. But he'da found out pretty quick; Red was up front with Longmile, puttin' ice on that black eye. That just left two of us, and the cops had obviously told him we were moonin' in black and white."

Luke asked anxiously, "You gonna tell?"

Third snorted, "Hell, naw. You sonuvagun, I'll be takin' the heat for you again! Naw, I just gotta see who wants to take the blame for the black butt -- I guess Buzz. No sense in everybody gettin' in Dutch with Daddy." He kicked another dry cow pie.

The CF Kid giggled. "I hope you feel like it's worth it. You shoulda seen that ole woman's face!" He and Third laughed together. "She looked like she'd swallered a frog! And then that... that ole lawyer, Daddy says he was, near'bout ran off the road! And then...."

"And then they pulled back up to see some more!" howled the towhead, holding his sides. The brothers collapsed beside the fence into their yard, laughing together, until Luke started coughing.

Longmile approached Mr. Leroy's office door softly, and pitched his hat in before knocking. "Bossman?"

The farmer reached for the drink machine key, tossing it and the hat back to the coach. While Longmile went for the drinks, Mr. Leroy pulled a pint bottle from the file drawer and took a pull, grimacing. They each drained a quarter of their colas, filled the bottles back up with the clear liquid, and shook the contents up with their thumbs over the tops of their bottles.

"The Barebutt Dodgers!" toasted Mr. Leroy.

"Moons over Alabama!" returned Longmile.

"What the hell was goin' on?" asked the team owner.

The coach took another pull at his bottle and wiped his mouth. "Ahh! Well, sir, I done got to the bottom of it, I think. Hump said he and Third mooned 'em when they wouldn't dim their lights and were drivin' too close to the bus. And there was a car back there for a while drivin' too close with brights on, so they're probably tellin' the truth. I recall thinkin' the guy was drunk, 'cause he was swervin' all over the road, but I didn't realize he was gettin' mooned! Lawd, Mr. Leroy, reckon what them kids'll think of next?"

"No tellin'!" the farmer exclaimed. "What'd you do about it so far?"

"Aw, I gave Hump a couple of licks, and he's writin' a letter of apology. Buzz is gonna write one as captain of the team. What about Third?"

Mr. Leroy shook his head. "He's damn near too big to be paddlin', but I gave him a couple of licks, too, and took the car keys away for a couple weeks. He's already called the lawyer and eaten crow. Did a pretty good job of calmin' things down. I could hardly keep from laughin' while he was talkin' to the wife. Of course," he added hastily, "Third's mama don't know about it yet. She'd throw a hissy fit, did she know."

Longmile nodded soberly, "Yessir. I told all the Dodgers to keep it to themselves. And Uncle Eb got onto 'em pretty hot and heavy. I got an idea he'll light into 'em for Sunday School next time!" He lifted an eyebrow at his employer, barely curbing a smile. "Mr. Leroy, you shoulda seen that guy goin' all over the road! And when he passed me finally, his wife's eyes was big as hen's eggs! I didn't know what the hell...." He smashed a thick palm on the desk and broke out laughing, joined by his companion.

In their room that night, Luke had just cut out the light

when he finally broached the subject. "Third, how'd it go this afternoon?"

His brother smiled in the dark. "Aw, Daddy gave me a lick or two, but you could tell he really wanted to laugh off the whole thing. I called and apologized. You'da been proud of me; butter wouldn't have melted in my mouth."

"Hump get by okay?"

"About the same. Longmile gave him a couple of half-hearted swats with a belt and told him to keep his britches up. He's writin' a letter to 'em, and so is Buzz, from the team."

"How come Hump instead of Buzz, takin' the blame?"

"We figured it'd put Daddy and Longmile in the position of havin' to defend us, since we were their boys. If Buzz had taken the heat, Longmile might have benched him or something, but he ain't fixin' to bench Hump!"

"So, nobody knows who started it, really?" Luke sounded somewhat relieved.

"You owe me, Luke, just remember that. You and Brown Brother shined your butts first and got plumb away with it!"

"Hey, you mooned 'em, too!" The CF Kid protested.

Third grinned to himself. "Not as much as you did! And if those Alabama folks ever found out exactly just how many blacks mooned 'em that night, they'd send the National Guard over here!"

The brothers laughed into their pillows. "Thanks, Third," Luke finally choked out, coughing.

"Oh, my goodness, Daddy! You mean somebody MOONED 'em?" Third mimicked, muffling his hilarity in the bedclothes.

"Shut up...and get me...my oxygen," The CF Kid laughed.

TEAM *Barefoot Dodgers*   RECORD   TEAM   RE

NO.	PLAYERS	B/A	POS/INN	1	2	3	4	5	6
1	Willy B / Brown Zuo	RF RF	A⁴₆			1-3	F9		
2	Jimmy Lee / Sherman	1B 2B	4						
3	Buzz / III	P 1B	10/4 6			F7		F7	
4	Hump	C			F8		E6		
5	Caleb	LF		6ᵏ			F8		
6	Spider	SS		L-4-3			6-3		
7	Rafe / Hay-Sue	CF CF	P₄ 4		5-3	3-4			
8	Junior / Luke / Red	3B	BN₅ PR₅	F9	4-3	4			
9	Blue Daddy / Wilbur	2B 2B	P₆		K				
Coach - Longmile									
UMPIRE Uncle Eb				4 3	3 2	1 1	1 0		
UMPIRE				LOB / ER	LOB / ER	LOB / ER	LOB / ER	LOB / ER	LOB / ER
UMPIRE				E	E	E	E	E	E
SCORER				D/p		D/p			

Chapter Twenty-Three

Only a week separated the IAL Regionals from the National Championships in St. Louis, but it was a week filled with frenzied activity. Mr. Leroy made hotel reservations for a block of ten rooms and rented a second school bus to transport anyone from Brownspur who wanted to attend. "Y'all just hafta buy your own meals," he decreed to the crowded commissary store that Saturday. Since there was very little plantation work that had to be done in August, several families signed up to go.

Longmile drilled his team each afternoon, concentrating mainly on infield combinations. Hey-Sue being his only substitute, the coach had to find the different positions each player could perform well at, "just in case someone gets hurt," he cautioned. The simultaneous losses of Jimmy Lee, Junior, and Wilber seriously limited the option of substitution. Hump was persuaded to loan his equipment to Hey-Sue, though begrudgingly, and the young Mexican was surprisingly good behind the plate. It was the first time Willy B had ever seemed remotely friendly to Hey-Sue, complimenting him with, "Man, you can sho' have that catcher's mitt if Hump gets taken out. I can't get off a throw near'bout as quick as you can, and if Rafe gets wild, I ain't got a prayer back there!"

Wilber was begged to return to the team, now that his baby was safely born, but he was steadfast at having "hung up his cleats," even though he had never owned a set of cleats. "Sarah needs me more'n ever now," he declared, "what with one nursin' and two underfoot. Y'all done fine without me in Birmingham," he pointed out correctly.

The fact that the Barefoot Dodgers had won the Southern Regional while playing white boys had attracted a great deal of media attention, as well as the animosity of the IAL officials, who spent the week seeking legal counsel in an effort to keep the National Championships all black. Mr. Leroy had wisely taken the league papers to his own attorney, however, who agreed with Longmile that nothing in them "discriminated against race, color, or creed." In his opinion, "They can change it next year to be all black or all green, but this year, all that makes any difference is that the players be listed on the original roster and be between the ages of fifteen and nineteen." Just in case, Mr. Leroy obtained a written opinion for Longmile to carry to St. Louis, where they both anticipated a challenge.

Professional umpires were to be provided at the Nationals, but Uncle Eb was included as an assistant coach, and would stay with the team. Had he not been able to go, Longmile was convinced that the Dodgers would not stand a chance. "You our good luck charm!" he told the elderly man. Indeed, most of the team felt the same way.

Both Buzz and Rafe had been approached by major league scouts during the Regional Tournament, and were so excited that Longmile began to doubt their efficiency should he start them pitching. "Look," the coach rumbled, "Y'all just got discovered in Birmingham. Get to thinkin' you're high and mighty in St. Louis, and you'll be hoein' cotton when you're seventy!"

"Le's just have fun, boys," Uncle Eb instructed. "We gonna teach them yankee niggers how to play ball!"

"Uncle Eb," Third queried, "Daddy won't let us say 'nigger'; how come it's all right for you to?"

The old man grinned, "If you're a nigger, you can call another nigger a nigger and nobody takes offense. Kinda like you callin' another white guy a redneck, but he'd get mad if I called him one."

"I don't get mad at y'all callin' me a peckerwood," Red observed.

"Chile, tha's just 'cause of your name.'Red-headed pecker Wood' fits you like the bird. You's red on the head, and you always peckin' at folks to make 'em mad."

"And you took out that Coonie catcher like he was a dead tree, too," Hump laughed. "Then he made you a blackeyed red-headed peckerwood!"

Brown Brother spoke up, "If Mr. Leroy hadn't grabbed me, I'da cleaned that catcher's plow for him. That sho' was a good fight!" he declared admiringly.

"Daddy's got the television station sendin' a tape of that to him," Luke said. "Matter of fact, they filmed most of the last two games. We can watch ourselves on teevee, soon as it gets here."

Longmile grunted. "Huh! Teevee and movie stars and prizefighters and major league wannabees. Y'all ain't gonna be worth shootin' time we get to St. Louis, your heads gonna be so big. Might as well send a note up there sayin' 'wasn't no sense in us showin' up, y'all woulda had us in your pockets.' Y'all better get your feet on the ground, or them city boys gonna send you home lookin' for a sugar-tit."

Buzz stood. "Nawsir. We goin' up there to play better ball than we did in Birmingham. And, Third, Luke, Red, Hey-Sue: I wanta say right now I was proud y'all was on the Barefoot Dodgers! Y'all done good, and I'm glad you was with us."

Hump and Blue chimed in, "Me too!" and Spider nodded in agreement. Brown Brother put his arm around Luke's shoulders. Caleb signaled "okay," as Rafe gave a thumbs-up. Third had just opened his mouth to speak when Willy B stood up.

"I gotta admit I never felt like it would work, y'all playin' with us blacks. Wasn't for it atall. But it worked out okay, and I gotta eat crow. Red, I wouldn't take a pretty for you takin' out that catcher; Third, you pitched great; Luke, you hit that homer so far, they're still lookin' for it; and Hey-Sue turned in a mighty nice double play to boot. We lookin' good in black and white!"

"Aw right," Longmile grunted. "Hit the field for practice. Y'all can congratulate one another after we win in St. Louis. But just remember," he cautioned, "those yankee teams been playin' together in this league for a long time. It's gonna be tougher than in Birmingham." He turned to Third. "And tougher on y'all, especially!"

Chapter Twenty-Four

Longmile had to fight the first battle for his white boys. When he arrived at the ballpark in St. Louis the day before the Series was to start, the International Amateur League officials and several coaches were assembled to greet him. The northern regional champs were coached by his old teammate, John Henry Vester, who had been the IAL contact who recruited the Barefoot Dodgers for league participation. The fact that Coach Vester had signed up the team which allowed white players had caused him no end of grief during the past week, for in an effort to assign blame, he was allotted the next largest share, right behind Longmile.

Greetings had scarcely been exchanged when Coach Vester tied into Longmile. "You knew when you signed up that this was a black league! How come you to put them white boys on your roster? We might come after you for fraud, if this IAL lawyer can find somethin' to hang you on!"

Longmile stood eye to eye with the irate coach. "Sure I knew that IAL had always been black! I ain't said that. What I'm sayin' is that it ain't nothin' in writin' says that, and I lost four players in a month. We ain't playin' whites 'cause we want to, we playin' 'em 'cause we got to! You knew we was a small team when you signed us up back last spring. And you watched us practice with those same white boys before our games. I bet every plantation team in the south got white boys that practice with 'em, and the Arkansas team we beat last week had played some games this year with a white catcher, and nobody said nothin'. Point here is, we wouldn't be here -- hell, we couldn't have played in the southern regionals -- without our whites, and there ain't nothin' in IAL rules sayin' they can't play."

The IAL president, a former major league all-star shortstop, stepped between the two. "Listen, Coach Henderson, we know there ain't nothin' in the rules -- Lord knows we've had enough lawyers look at them in the past couple weeks -- but, man, you got every newspaper and television network in the country worked up about this thing. Now they're sayin' we're tryin' to discriminate against the whites, and we understand the ACLU has even contacted your plantation owner about goin' to court. It's put us in a bad light. If we try to correct it next year, the ACLU says it damn well will sue us. You realize you could be the death of the IAL all by yourself?"

Uncle Eb held up a hand. "Ain't no need to go to cussin' over this, mister. We all s'posed to be friends and baseball lovers here. This league is for the kids, and belongs to be run for them. Down south, we been used to whites and blacks bein' separated except for friendship forever, and a lotta that's been changed in the past fifteen years, for better or worse. Some of y'all come down south to help get black kids in white schools and clubs and the fronta the bus. Now you gonna tell us you ain't wantin' to play with whites up here? Man, you wouldn'ta made no money atall if they'd kept the old Negro League and still had just whites in the majors. Hadn'ta been for Jackie Robinson, you'da been shinin' shoes down at the railroad station! Tell me you ain't in favor of integration!"

"Well, I am thataway," the president protested. "But...."

"No buts!" Longmile instructed. "You played with whites in the majors, just like John Henry did, and y'all are mighty proud of it! Now, put your money where your mouth is. I didn't sign up in thishere league to make trouble, and didn't ask for four players to get hurt. If y'all had rules for substitutes to the rosters, I'da picked some blacks. But the Barefoot Dodgers won the state fair and square with all blacks, and won the southern fair and square with blacks and whites. You goin' backward? We gonna have another Civil War over this?"

"You betcha!" the angry Coach Vester declared. "Don't let them white boys get in our way, or you'll be carryin' 'em off feet first. You ain't s'posed to be playin' whites, Longmile, and my guys are gonna make 'em wish they'd never seen a baseball!"

Quicker than a snake, Longmile's hand flashed out to grab the coach's shirtfront. "Lemme tell you somethin', John Henry. You was mean when we played together, and you ain't changed a nickel's worth. Well, if one of my boys gets hurt -- and they're ALL my boys, black or white -- I'm gonna jump down your throat and ball the jack on your gizzard!" He looked at the IAL president as he shoved the offending coach back in disgust. "Bubba, you heard this SOB threaten my players; if one of mine gets hurt, I'm puttin' you on notice right now that my boss will sue the IAL. You better tell your umps that we come to play baseball, not fight. And if someone starts anything, I want your word that they'll be outa the game superquick!" He turned back to his original target. "And John Henry, I mean it about kickin' your tail. I done it before, and I'll do it again!"

The league attorney stepped in before anyone could respond. "All right, that's enough! Coach, you made a threat before witnesses that may endanger the league," he told Vester. "Put a lid on it. There ain't a damn thing we can do about this situation except play ball -- and good, clean, hard ball! We got television cameras, newspapers, magazines, and major league scouts here to cover this series, and if your boys -- either of your boys, of any color -- play dirty, it'll be in every household on the ten o'clock news. We've already been made fools of in this thing. Let's don't be made damn fools!"

"Ain't no call for cussin'," Uncle Eb reminded again. "The Bible says to call no man a fool, especially a damn fool. But lemme tell y'all what you may be missin' here; the most important thing of all." He pointed toward the pressbox upstairs, then swept his hand to encompass the field outside. "I ain't never seen the IAL in print or screen before. Never woulda heard of it except I was connected with a ball team that played some IAL teams in the past. Never knew how big the IAL was until John Henry came down and talked us into signing up for the league. I bet the same thing's true for ninety-five percent of the population of these United States, where baseball is s'posed to be the national pasttime."

He paused for effect. "But in the past week or so, the IAL has been on every teevee network, written up in most newspapers, and you've gotten more publicity out of three white boys and a Mexican than you've gotten in twenty years, combined." The league president and attorney glanced meaningfully at each other as the old man's point struck home. "Y'all gonna have more applications for teams in the next month than you've ever had. You want to double your size? Go west? Really be international? Here's your chance." He pointed at the lawyer, "Who pays your retainer? You get more for the more work you have to do?" He wheeled to the president, "Who pays your salary? You want more, for more responsibility?"

Again he swept his arm toward the field. "How many scouts are gonna get sent to IAL teams next year, 'cause now they know more about you? How many kids are gonna get a major league shot they never woulda had, except for these Brownspur white boys? How many college educations are gonna be offered to black boys 'cause coaches went to see them play?" He ended his oration by reaching into his pocket for a plug of tobacco, but his audience still sat in silence, even Longmile shocked by Uncle Eb's vehemence. Just as he started to bite, he stopped and said, almost sadly, "You wanta be big time? Stop thinkin' like a bunch of prejudiced Ku Kluxers...."

The attorney turned to the president, who still sat openmouthed. "Jesus, he's right! You know that?"

"Was that a cussword?" Uncle Eb asked suspiciously.

"No, sir," the lawyer said respectfully. "That was a prayer!"

TEAM **Barefoot Dodgers** RECORD TEAM RE

NO.	PLAYERS	B/A	POS INN	1	2	3	4	5	6
1	Willy B	RF				1-3 F9			
	SUB. Bram Bro	RF	PH6						
2	Jimmy Lee	1B							
	SUB. Sherman	2B	4	E3	61	RBI			
3	Buzz	P	1B 4			F7		F7	
	SUB. III	1B	6						
4	Hump	C			F8 RBI			E6 RBI	
	SUB.								
5	Caleb	LF		6-K				F8	
	SUB.								
6	Spider	SS		6,4-3			RBI	6-3	
	SUB.								
7	Rafe	CF	P4		5-3	3-4			
	SUB. Hay-Sue	CF	4						
8	Junior	3B		F9		4-3	4		
	SUB. Luke		PH5						
	SUB. Red	3B	P5						
9	Blue Daddy	2B			K				
	SUB. Wilbur	2B	P6				2 RBI		
	SUB.								
	SUB.								
	Coach - Longmile								
	SUB.								
	SUB.								
UMPIRE Uncle Eb				R 4 H 3	R 3 H 2	R 1 H 1	R 1 H 0	R H	R
UMPIRE				LOB 1 / ER 1	LOB 2 / ER 1	LOB 1 / ER 0	LOB 1 / ER	LOB / ER	LOB
UMPIRE				E	E	E	E	E	E
SCORER				0/0		0/0			

The Barefoot Dodgers

Chapter Twenty-Five

In that spirit, the IAL president asked Uncle Eb to begin the games with a prayer, something that had not been done before, but was common in the south. The president had already spoken to both teams, the Barefoot Dodgers and the Mansfield Maulers, about the importance of fair play and clean baseball. Uncle Eb hit it again in his beseeching: "Oh Lord, we ask your blessings upon this series. Keep these boys safe from injury. Give the coaches and umpires wisdom and vision to make the right calls. Keep us all -- players, coaches, umps, and fans -- mindful of the fact that you loves us all -- black, white, brown, red, or yellow -- and gave your Son to die for all of us that we might be saved from our sins. Lord," and this was delivered rather sternly, Longmile thought, "Don't let none of us sin on this baseball field by cheatin', lyin', name-callin', or hurtin' one another. Let each play to the best of the talents that You have given him, and we thank You for a country where we can all play ball together. Amen."

The pre-game ceremonies took quite a while longer than anticipated, since for the first time, there was television coverage of an IAL Series. Not only were there signaled commercial breaks, but each participant seemed to make the most of his or her time before the camera. The daughter of the St. Louis Cardinals first baseman, an accomplished singer, did the "Star Spangled Banner" and each player was introduced. During all this time, Mr. Leroy was casting an anxious eye at the skies. A fast-moving weather front was approaching from the west, and lightning flashed from the low black clouds.

"Be a shame for the game to get rained out after all this hullabaloo," he remarked to Uncle Eb.

Thunderclaps rumbled just west of the stadium, prompting

the president to signal to the home plate umpire. "Let me call the radio station and get an update before we start this thing," he suggested. Since the game time had already been delayed for nearly half an hour by the ceremonies, the ump agreed.

Minutes later, he was passed the word that there were indeed severe weather watches out, and a tornado had been sighted north of the city. The umpires, coaches, and officials huddled, and agreed to further delay the start of the game. Both teams had taken warmups, and Buzz was throwing easily to Hump in the bullpen. Longmile waved everyone into the dugout. "Looks like we gotta storm comin' in, boys," he noted. "Keep your arm loose, Buzz, and don't anybody get tight, but we're gonna delay the game to see what this front's gonna do."

"Sooner the better, Pop," Hump enthused. "Buzz is throwin' as good as he's ever thrown. I mean, that knuckler is doin' a dance! We don't wanta get this one called for rain."

And it wasn't. The game was delayed for twenty minutes, but the front had apparently stalled just west of town. "Shoot," Coach Vester exclaimed, "It might stay there the rest of the afternoon. Let's at least start."

Another huddle was held, eyes cast toward the dark clouds roiling behind home plate, but seemingly halted for the time being. Finally, the head umpire signaled, "Play ball!" and the Mansfield Maulers took the field. Willy B stepped to the plate, with Spider on deck.

The Mauler pitcher, Spike Wilson, was as hard-throwing as Rafe, with excellent control. Willy B took a strike, swung at another, fouled off six pitches, then tipped one that the catcher held on to. He flipped his helmet into the dugout in disgust. "That guy ain't thrown a ball yet!"

Lightning flashed closer as Spider took his stance in the box, and the umpire glanced behind him fearfully. "It gets any

The Barefoot Dodgers

closer, we're gonna get struck," he muttered to Charlie Perkins, the catcher, who grunted in agreement. Spider grinned easily.

"Y'all are safe, long as I'm up here. Tall as I am and holdin' a bat up, and y'all squatted down. Shoot, I'm like a lightnin' rod for y'all!" They all chuckled.

Spider wasn't chuckling when he walked back three pitches later, however. "That cat's throwin' smoke!" he declared.

Caleb took the first pitch for a strike, the thirteenth in a row from the Mauler ace. He backed out to knock dirt from his spikes. "When does he throw balls?" he asked the catcher.

"When he wants to!" was the discouraging reply.

The Dodger left fielder got all the way around on the next offering, though, and drilled it into the stands foul over third. That got him a ball for the next two pitches, both obviously placed just off the outside corner. "This guy's good," Caleb muttered, and readied himself for a decent pitch.

It was a fast ball low and away, and the Dodger got under it, with all his power, but too far under. It was one of those "mile-high" pop-ups. The second baseman drifted over and the center fielder came charging in, but the Mauler shortstop, Casey Potter, called for it, camping ten steps back of the bag.

And the front came through.

Suddenly, players' caps, fans' programs, empty drink cups, popcorn bags, and other items came blowing across the field. The St. Louis weather bureau later said the front had straight-line winds gusting up to fifty-five miles per hour. Caleb's pop-up was right at the height of its trajectory when the winds took it. Casey Potter watched openmouthed as the baseball sailed over the center field fence, clearing it by ten feet. The batter crossed home plate just as the hail hit and the umpires called time. Everyone ran for the dugout, the Barefoot Dodgers cheering wildly.

The game was delayed less than ten minutes. Having stalled

briefly just west of the city, the front moved quickly when it unstalled. A quick smattering of hail, barely enough rain to spot the basepaths, and then just low, scudding clouds followed the squall line. When the teams took the field again, there was a heated argument between the umpire and Coach Vester as to whether Caleb's pop-up homer should count. Actually, Longmile thought his opponent had a valid point, but loudly maintained that time had been called after the hit, so that the time-out did not commence until the play was over, which was what the rule books said, true enough. Vester quit just before getting thrown out, and play resumed with the Barefoot Dodgers leading by one to nothing. Hump grounded to short to end the inning.

And that was just about it. The first game of the IAL series was one of the best pitchers' duels ever seen, majors included. As Hump had declared, Buzz was at his best that day, his knuckler floating and dancing as the Maulers went down in frustration. On the other hand, Spike was nearly untouchable, and a Ranger scout with a radar gun clocked one pitch as high as 102 miles per hour.

In the sixth inning, Hump couldn't hold onto a third strike knuckler -- which was to be expected; Third at first had seven assists for the day, on strikeouts alone -- and the batter made it to first. The next Mauler sacrificed successfully, and there was a runner in scoring position with one out. Spike Wilson had a chance to help himself out, but grounded weakly back to Buzz, who looked the runner back at second, and fired to first for the out. But the Mauler baserunner broke when Buzz released the ball, and Third saw a chance for a double play. He quickly threw to Red covering, and the runner had only one chance -- to separate the third sacker from the ball. He came in cleats up, and Red was knocked over the base and into the coach's box, but he held onto the ball.

As the umpire called "Yer out!" Red tossed the ball at him and charged the runner, but both Buzz and Spider realized what was the likely outcome of the play, and anticipated Red's action. Tackled by his own teammates, Red was unable to get into a fray, though Mauler taunts from the bench infuriated him even more. He was half-carried to the dugout by Spider, bleeding from two cuts on his jaw, and Mr. Leroy wisely took the redhead to the hospital, where the emergency room doctor used four stitches to sew him up. Longmile moved Blue to third base, and sent Hey-Sue to second, with instructions to "Cool it!"

The game ended at one to nothing, Caleb's wind-blown pop-up being the only run. Mansfield had two scratch hits off Buzz, and the Barefoot Dodgers had managed only one other baserunner off Spike, an error by the first baseman on a throw from short on Third's grounder. Coach Vester placed a formal protest against counting Caleb's homer, but it was denied. Uncle Eb voiced the thought of the day: "Boys, the good Lord just wanted y'all to win today!"

A baseball scorecard for the Barefoot Dodgers.

NO.	PLAYERS	B/A	POS/INN	1	2	3	4	5	6
1	Willy B	RF				1-3	F9		
	SUB. Brown Slu	RF	P4/6						
	SUB.								
2	Jimmy Lee	1B							
	SUB. Sherman	2B	4						
	SUB.			E3	61	RBI			
3	Buzz	P	1B/4			F7	F7		
	SUB. III		1B 6						
	SUB.								
4	Hump	C			F8			E6	
	SUB.								
	SUB.				RBI			RBI	
5	Caleb	LF		6-4				F8	
	SUB.								
	SUB.								
6	Spider	SS		6-4-3			6-3		
	SUB.						RBI		
	SUB.								
7	Rafe	CF	P4		5-3	3-4			
	SUB. Hay-Sue	CF	4						
	SUB.								
8	Junior	3B		F9	4-3	K			
	SUB. Luke		P4/5						
	SUB. Red	3B	P4/5						
9	Blue Daddy	2B			K				
	SUB. Wilbur	4th	2B P6			2 RBI			
	SUB.								
	SUB.								
	SUB.								
	Coach - Longmile								
	SUB.								
	SUB.								
UMPIRE Uncle Eb				R4 3	R3 2	R1 1	R1 0		
UMPIRE				LOB1 ER	LOB2 ER	LOB1 0 ER	LOB1 ER	LOB ER	LOB
UMPIRE				E	E	E	E	
SCORER				B/P	B/P			

TEAM Barefoot Dodgers   RECORD   TEAM

Chapter Twenty-Six

The International Amateur League Championship Series was a best three of five games series, one game a day over five days. Longmile had decided to follow the same pitching rotation that had proven so successful in the regionals. Rafe started the second game, and Hump cast an anxious eye at his father after warming the hard-throwing righty up in the bullpen prior to game time. "He's a little wild right now," the catcher whispered.

And so he was. Rafe walked the first two batters for the Maulers, and only a sharply hit well-handled wormburner to Spider saved him with a double play. The cleanup hitter had to duck two pitches, and backed up in the box too far to get good wood on a fastball on the outside corner, which he dribbled down to Third at first. Hump consoled Charlie Perkins, his counterpart in both catching and cleaning up, "Man, tell your guys to be loose up here until he settles down some. He usually ain't this wild but for a couple of innings."

John Henry Vester, however, complained loudly to the umpire that Rafe was throwing beanballs. To which the ump replied, "Coach, he's just as wild on t'other side of the plate!"

The Mauler pitcher was long and lanky, taller even than Buzz, and threw in a similar style, except that he came from the left side. Treetop Smiley had secured a college scholarship for his basketball talents, but did not play baseball at school, so therefore was eligible for competition under IAL rules. He set down the Barefoot Dodgers in order in the bottom of the first, using only seven pitches in the process. "You gotta wait on those slow curves," Longmile warned his players.

Rafe staggered through three scoreless innings in spite of his wildness before being touched for two runs in the fourth.

Two hit batsmen, two walks, and a dying quail barely over Blue Daddy's glove brought Longmile to the mound. "Reckon I better bring Third in?" the coach asked his frustrated hurler.

"C'mon, Coach, gimme a chance. I feel like I'm fixin' to get it grooved," Rafe begged. He looked to Hump for support, and the catcher nodded loyally.

"Those guys he hit were crowdin' the plate pretty good, sho'nuff," Hump acknowledged. "But, Rafe, maybe you oughta rest up for awhile. Those two you walked weren't crowdin' nothin'. You got 'em scared, but can't hit the corners."

The pitcher had a pleading look in his eyes. "Longmile, there's a dozen pro scouts in the stands. Don't jerk me, please!"

"Uh-huh. I kinda figured that's what you was doin'. Now you lissen here. I'll leave you in, but you quit worryin' about the guys in the stands and start worryin' about the guys in the box! You concentrate on Hump's mitt, you hear?"

"Yessir. Hump's mitt. You got it, Coach. Thanks."

The next six pitches were strikes, only two swinging. As the second batter swung and missed, Hump fired unexpectedly to first base, where Third had slipped in behind the runner. The inning was over, but the Dodgers were down by two runs.

Spider tripled in the sixth, a blooper down the right field line, and Buzz brought him home on a suicide squeeze. However, in the bottom of that inning, Rafe served up a gopher ball to Charlie Perkins, who parked the ball deep in the left field seats. That rattled the Dodger pitcher, who walked the next man on four balls in a row that Hump had to block. The catcher came to the mound, to be joined by the infielders. "C'mon, Rafe, you got to get it together, man. You want Third to take over?"

The blonde first baseman patted his pitcher's shoulder. "C'mon, fella, suck it up and get tough. Let's save me for tomorrow. Just look at the mitt. You can do it!"

The righty took a deep breath. "Okay, Hump, just one more. Lemme get this guy out. If I can't, Third can have it. Okay?"

The first two pitches were good fastballs, letter high, and the batter took one and missed the other. Rafe wasted one outside, and tried to get him to go fishing for a high changeup, but the Mauler resisted. On a two-two count, the slider hung and the bat cracked, sending a vicious one-hopper deep to Spider's left. The shortstop smothered it, picked it up barehanded, and fired to first, seeing that the runner was too close to second for a force. His hurried throw was high, and while Third's leap snared the ball, he was in the air over the bag when the Mauler runner arrived. There was no doubt that the runner was safe, and that he could have missed the Dodger first sacker, but as he crossed the bag, he swung a forearm and shoulder into the descending white boy. Third was knocked head over heels into the dust.

Longmile and Uncle Eb were out of the dugout and running at the impact, the former to see to the health of his first baseman, and the latter to corral Hump before he flattened the runner. Thinking quickly, Luke screamed "Time!" before the Maulers advanced on the basepaths. Blue Daddy grabbed Rafe, who also had revenge in mind, and Willy B tackled Buzz, who was racing in from center with a vengeful eye. Longmile helped the groggy Third to sit up, and inspected a lump already half the size of an egg on the back of the boy's head. Spider kneeled beside them, and Luke bent over his brother. "You gonna be okay, Third? Anything busted? Your arm move all right?"

The blonde head shook slowly, and when it raised, Third's eyes were obviously out of focus. "Man, what a lick," he muttered thickly.

Longmile stood to see the runner standing on first with a slight smirk on his face, and John Henry Vester grinning in the first base coaches' box. "That white boy's head ain't as hard as you thought, is it?" the Mauler coach asked.

"I warned you," the stocky ex-catcher hissed as he stalked toward his former teammate, fists balled up. Coach Vester's mistake was in not taking Longmile seriously. His guard was down as he thrust his head forward to argue with his counterpart, but Longmile was past arguing.

Caleb was still in left field, but clearly heard the crack of fist upon jaw just as if a wooden bat had connected with a home run shot. John Henry Vester went down like a poled ox.

"Yer outa the game!!" the umpire bellowed at Longmile. "Hell, I might throw you out of the series for that! You deliberately hit...."

"I told him and I told you what'd happen if y'all started playin' rough and dirty!" Longmile was right up in the ump's face, fists still clenched. The IAL president and lawyer appeared, running from the press box.

"Grab that crazy sonuvabitch! This is on teevee!" the attorney yelled.

By now, Leroy Alexander had decided his presence was called for to calm down his coach. He ran to grasp Longmile's arm before the umpire received the same treatment, as Uncle Eb clasped him from the other side. "Yer outa here!" the ump screamed again. Mr. Leroy dragged the furious coach off the field by brute force, helped by Uncle Eb.

The stands had erupted into noise, much of it abuse directed toward the downed first baseman. "Hey, white boy, how you like them apples?" "Atta way to show 'em, Maulers!" "Get up, honkie! Can't take a little bump?" The Mauler dugout emptied, many of the players taunting the Brownspur whites with like jibes. Red Wood threw his glove and balled his fists.

Luke by now had helped the woozy Third to his feet, and was attempting to hold an enraged Red with the other hand.

"Hey-Sue, help!" he called to the Mexican. "Brown Brother, c'mere!" He delivered his brother to these two and shoved Red backwards into Spider's arms. "Calm down!" he ordered. The Barefoot Dodgers bunched up stiffly, obviously ready to fight. The IAL officials ran between the teams, trying to restore order. A black doctor retained by the League for the tournament knelt in front of Third, as Mr. Leroy returned to the field. "How is he?" an anxious Luke asked the physician.

"You his daddy?" the doctor addressed Mr. Leroy.

"Right. Is he okay? Third, can you talk? How you feel?"

The towhead gamely tried to shake off the effects of the collision. "I'll be okay. Gimme a minute." But his knees were too obviously wobbly.

"Mister, he's got a pretty good knot on his head and his eyes are dilated. I believe he might have a mild concussion. If you want to take him to a hospital, it might be wise, just to let them look him over. That's a fine lump."

"Right. C'mon, son. I know where it is, since I took Red yesterday. Thanks, Doc." He shook hands with the physician.

"You need me, Daddy?" Luke asked.

"Nah. I think he's okay. I'll take your momma; you stay with the team and calm these guys down. But don't YOU get in a scrap! You hear me?"

"Yessir. Hang in there, Third."

The League officials and umpires had succeeded in clearing the field. Coach Vester had been helped to his dugout, and an ice pack applied to his jaw. Longmile had reappeared in the stands behind first base, still trying to control his temper, and being talked to by the IAL president. The Barefoot Dodgers began to move back to their positions when the umpire called, "Play Ball!" But then Uncle Eb, now the Dodger coach, noticed the runner still on first.

"Hey, Ump!" the old man called, walking toward home plate. "That guy on first was out for intentionally hitting my fielder."

"I didn't see it thataway," the first base umpire stated, trotting down the line to meet Uncle Eb. "The fielder was in the air over the bag when the runner crossed."

The Barefoot Dodgers had never seen Uncle Eb mad before. He drew himself up and bellowed in the umpire's face, "He hit my man on purpose! You gotta call him out!"

"I'll call YOU out, you old sonuvabitch!" the head umpire declared. "Yer out!" and he pointed toward the stands. As he did so, Longmile stood, doubling his fists, but the League president pulled him back down.

"You gonna let that guy stay on first?" Uncle Eb asked softly.

"Yeah. And you're gone, old fella!"

"I mought be old, but I know the rules and I don't cuss. Where I come from, we wouldn't let you call hogs!"

Luke appeared to pull Uncle Eb away, for now the Barefoot Dodgers were gathering around Rafe at the mound, and the Maulers were advancing again from their dugout. Caleb grabbed Uncle Eb's other arm. "C'mon, Daddy. Let 'im be. Let's play ball."

As team captain, Buzz took command. "Luke, you're manager now. Take over. Want me to pitch, or what?"

The CF Kid released Uncle Eb as Caleb led him toward the gate behind first. "Well....I guess I'm the only one left, huh? Y'all c'mere." He motioned for the Dodgers to gather at the mound. "Aw right, y'all ready to play baseball? Rafe, can you throw strikes now? Lord knows you've had a rest here!"

There were a couple of slight grins, as Luke's joke broke the tension. "Lemme stay for a while, Luke....Coach Luke."

Luke nodded. "But we can't afford no more walks or hit

batters. And lissen, you guys. We can't have nobody else gettin' hurt or thrown out. Keep it cool and let's get this one over with and get the taste out of our mouths." He looked at the Mexican. "Hey-Sue, take left field; Caleb, you're in center; Buzz, you're on first. Don't get in anybody's way!" He clapped his hands. "Let's play ball!"

TEAM _Barefoot Dodgers_ RECORD TEAM RE...

NO.	PLAYERS	B/A	POS/INN	1	2	3	4	5	6
1	Willy B	RF				1-3	F9		
	SUB. Brown Bro	RF	PH6						
2	Jimmy Lee	1B							
	SUB. Sherman	2B	4	E3	61	RBI			
3	Buzz	P	1B/4			F7		F7	
	SUB. III	1B	6						
4	Hump	C			F8		E6		
	SUB.				RBI		RBI		
5	Caleb	LF		6-4				F8	
6	Spider	SS		6-4-3			6-3		
	SUB.					RBI			
7	Rafe	CF	P4		5-3	3-4			
	SUB. Hay-Sue	CF	4						
8	Junior	3B		F9		4-3	4		
	SUB. Luke		PH5						
	SUB. Red	3B	PR5						
9	Blue Daddy	2B			K				
	SUB. Wilbur 4th	2B	P6			2 RBI			
	SUB.								
	Coach - Longmile								
UMPIRE _Uncle Eb_				4 3	3 2	1 1	1 0		
UMPIRE				LOB1 / 1ER	LOB2 /	LOB1 / 0ER	LOB1 / ER	LOB / ER	LOB /
UMPIRE				E	E	E	E	E	E
SCORER				B/p		B/p			

150 The Barefoot Dodgers

Chapter Twenty-Seven

Slowly, the game began again, after a half-hour delay. Luke asked for a few warmup pitches and the umpire obliged. The white boy reported his lineup changes to the other dugout, introducing himself: "Coach Vester, I'm Coach Alexander. How's your jaw?" His answer was a muffled grunt.

Finally, the Mauler hitter stepped to the plate, and the umpire once again called, "Play Ball!" Rafe immediately picked off the runner at first. It was a close play, but Buzz got the call, though the runner argued vehemently. "Son, I ain't in the mood," the ump warned with a glint in his eye. Coach Vester rose and started from the dugout, more in loyalty to his player than in dedication to the cause. The man in blue stopped him with, "Coach, cross that line and you're gone!" Vester retreated.

Rafe's first pitch to the plate was not a strike. It was an inside fast ball -- a high inside fast ball. Casey Potter barely missed being struck by the missile, and the Mauler dugout emptied as their captain and shortstop arose, grabbed his bat, and headed for the mound. The umpire and Luke headed him off. "Hold it, man. He's been wild all game. He wasn't throwing at you," Luke tried to soothe.

The umpire tended to agree with the batter. "I think he tried to bean him," he declared. "Mr. Pitch,...." But Luke interrupted.

"Ump, he's wild, and he's upset. I'll get him out. Buzz, take the mound; Rafe, center field -- now!" the young coach forestalled any argument. He waved Hey-Sue in to take second, Caleb over into left, and Blue Daddy to first. "Lemme warm up a new pitcher, Ump," he stated firmly.

Once again, a confrontation threatened. The Maulers bunched on the third base line, ready to back their captain, who stood halfway to the mound. Red Wood had positioned himself in front of Casey Potter, and Spider was next to him. Caleb came trotting in from left, as did Willy B from right. Only Hey-Sue and Rafe remained at their assigned positions. The air was electric; even the umpire realized that a spark would start a fight. Into the breech stepped the CF Kid.

"Looka here," the white boy stared up at the Mauler captain, "You know and I know that this is gettin' outa hand. Now lemme tell you somethin'. All this started because a couple of our guys have gotten hurt in two games. One was maybe a good hard clean play, but this last one was dirty. Both our guys to get hurt were white, one my brother.

"Now, lissen: we didn't ask to play with the Barefoot Dodgers in this series, but we been raised with all these guys, and played together for years. We got a small team, but a good team, and won the state with black players. But we've lost three guys to accidents, and one to havin' a baby. It was just an accident we white boys were on the roster, and an accident that it ain't in League rules that just blacks can play.

"So, it's just by accident that some of us of another color are here...but we didn't come here to fight about anything, much less about race. We came here to play baseball. We came to kick your tails fair and square on the baseball field, not fight...but if we gotta fight, then y'all just say the word and we'll all get a bat and settle this right now, win, lose, or draw!

"We might not can beat you fightin', 'cause there's more of y'all than us. But if that's what you want, jump right in."

Luke was beginning to breathe harshly, and his voice rattled in his throat. Buzz edged closer as he noticed his young coach's face beginning to redden. Yet Luke wasn't through and his audience knew it. After a short coughing spell, he began again.

"We came up here to play baseball, and we think we can

beat you fair and square, if you play that way. But if you guys are gonna play dirty -- and you know you took my brother out on purpose," he leveled a finger at the offending Mauler, "then let's get it right out front. Be man enough to say you're gonna cheat to win!" he challenged Casey, breathing heavily. Once more he stooped to cough heavily, hawking and spitting phlegm. Red-faced, he continued, shaking off Buzz's warning hand.

"But I b'lieve you're better than that. I b'lieve you're man enough to shake my hand and say you'll try to beat us fair and clean. If you play clean to win, we got no problem. If you gotta play dirty to beat us, that means we're better'n you -- and you know it!" He extended his hand to the Mauler captain.

Potter hesitated. No one had talked to him like that in years. He glanced over his shoulder at his teammates, but not for confirmation of his answer; just for confirmation that he was their leader. Frowning, he grasped Luke's hand. "We can kick y'all's tails fair and square," he growled. "And we'll play it that way, white boy. You got my word."

Luke nodded solemnly. "Fine. You got mine too," he choked out, and spat sideways again.

The umpire was almost meek in asking, "Y'all ready to play ball now?"

"Batter up!" Luke said, still shaking Casey Potter's hand.

Potter lined a knuckleball to Spider, who tagged the runner at second to double up and end the inning. The rest of the game was almost anticlimactic, both teams seemingly just wanting off the field. Third showed back up in the ninth, just in time to see Hey-Sue pop up weakly to second to end the game. The Dodgers crowded around the towhead, who had been pronounced all right except for that knot and a slight concussion, as diagnosed on the field. Coach Luke walked across to congratulate the Mauler captain, whose coach had retired early to the dressing room.

Casey once more shook the white boy's hand. "Thanks. Buy you a beer after we shower?"

Luke grinned, "Thanks, but I ain't old enough. See you on the field tomorrow. Lemme go check on my brother. Good game."

Buzz also had come over to congratulate the Maulers on their win. Potter cornered him. "Hey, man, sorry it got outa hand. That's a gutsy white boy you got there. Is somethin' wrong with him, coughin' like that?"

"He's got Cystic Fibrosis; his lungs fill up and he ain't s'posed to get hot. We have to watch out for him. Yeah, guts!"

"He gonna get over it?"

Buzz looked toward center field, and Casey Potter noticed that his eyes seemed to be misty. "Naw." And the Barefoot Dodger captain walked away.

Chapter Twenty-Eight

The two coaches glowered at each other as they exchanged lineups for the third game of the International Amateur League Championship Series. The IAL president beckoned the coaches and umpires into a huddle behind home plate. "Listen," he demanded, "you guys got to get a handle on things for the rest of these games. Look at the media folks here. That was a circus act yesterday that I won't stand for today. Ump," he instructed, "I want these players on a tight string. Anybody looks crosseyed, toss 'em out -- coaches, players, batboys, umpires -- I don't care who it is! Longmile, you and John Henry bury the hatchet, period. No rough stuff between you or your players, I don't care what color they are. Understand?"

Longmile scowled at the first base umpire. "Fine with me, as long as you guys don't allow any more cheap shots like you did yesterday. You call the game like it ought to be called, okay?"

The umpire in question started to bridle, but the president stood him down. "Bernie, he's right. You and I both know the runner hit that boy on purpose. Well, if you don't do your job today, I'll come down here and call it myself, you hear?"

Third was still somewhat affected by the concussion, though protesting mightily that he was fine, and Longmile made the decision not to start him pitching. "Okay, boys, here's how we're gonna work it: I'll start Buzz, let him go a couple of innings, then switch to Rafe for a couple, until they can't find the plate. As long as you both stay in the game, I can move you back and forth whenever I need to. Maybe we can keep them off balance thataway."

"You ain't gonna play me?" Third asked plaintively.

"Not startin' out. I ain't satisfied you're plumb okay yet. Go down in the bullpen and chunk with Brown Brother. Stay loose. After you work up a sweat, if you don't weak out on us, I'll think about lettin' you in. Blue, you take first to begin with, and Hey-Sue, you're on second."

Luke volunteered, "I'll play first if you want me to."

Willy B grinned, "You got pretty het up yesterday, Luke. Better let well enough alone. I'll fudge up a little to pick up the grounders that Hey-Sue and Blue Daddy miss."

Pitching on two days rest, Buzz was not exactly sharp, but neither was he flat. The Maulers touched him, but never got good wood on a ball but once, when a screaming liner got by Hey-Sue, who managed to knock it down, but couldn't field it cleanly. However, there were two outs and the next batter flied to left, so no damage was done.

The Maulers' pitcher was not as good as the two previous starters, and the Barefoot Dodgers got to him in the top of the third with three successive doubles by Caleb, Hump, and Buzz. Red then sacrificed to move the Dodger captain to third, and Buzz came home on a grounder to Casey Potter in deep short.

Rafe came on in the fourth to pitch, and obviously had not found the groove. He walked one, gave up a single to the next, and then Hey-Sue booted a double play. Willy B ran the ball into the infield, but runners were at the corners with one out and a run scored. "C'mon, man. Get down on the ball!" the right fielder growled to the Mexican.

The speedy little leadoff batter tagged Rafe's 3-2 offering, pulling it barely fair into the left field corner, where the ball took a weird bounce back past the charging Caleb and was finally chased down by Spider Webb, whose throw was slightly off the mark to Hump at the plate. It was an inside-the-park homer.

When the Dodgers finally ended the inning, they were down by two runs, and Willy B threw his glove into the dugout disgustedly. "Four unearned runs! Hell, let Brown Brother play second base, Longmile!"

"Can it!" the coach ordered. "Like you never made an error before? We're hittin' this guy good; let's just get some runs!"

The game seesawed back and forth, the lead exchanging hands several times. Buzz came back in to pitch the eighth with the score knotted at seven-all, to be greeted by a single. With the infield in, the batter drag bunted, and the ball was fielded by Blue Daddy, who hurried his throw to Hey-Sue covering first. A taller boy would have made the catch, but the young Mexican was only five-four, and could not glove the high throw, which went into the right field bullpen. Willy B hustled it in, but runners were at second and third, no outs. "Man, you look like a hog on ice out here!" he complained to Hey-Sue. "Get in the game!"

Blue Daddy corrected him, "My fault, guys. No sweat, Hey-Sue; nice try."

Buzz tried to calm down his right fielder. "Hey, it was a high throw, Willy B. I'da had trouble comin' up with that one."

"Right," was the sardonic reply. "Get with it, Spic!"

The next Mauler popped up a knuckler to Spider, and Buzz got a good call on a slow curve for a third strike on Casey Potter. Two outs; and the first pitch to the cleanup hitter was popped to shallow right. Hey-Sue backpedaled, shielding his eyes, as Willy B sprinted in. At the last second, Rafe in center realized that they were going to collide. "Willy! Willy!" he designated, but it was too late. The fielders crashed into each other and the ball rolled free. Both runners were moving, with two outs, and had scored when Rafe retrieved the baseball.

"Stupid Spic!" Willy B screamed. "That was my...."

And Hey-Sue collided with him again. The little Mexican tackled his accuser and the two rolled in the outfield grass, pummeling each other, as Buzz cried "Time!" and the Dodgers rushed to break up the fight. Everyone but Longmile. The coach smiled at Luke and grabbed his scorekeeper to keep him from rushing onto the field too.

"Told you that Mexican boy would finally get fed up with Willy B's lip. Now they'll get along. Let 'em be."

The umpires huddled briefly as the Barefoot Dodgers separated the combatants. "There's a rule about the teams fightin' each other, but not about amongst themselves," the home plate ump declared. "They're apart now. Let's play ball!"

A furious Buzz bore down and struck out the next batter to end the inning. Willy B approached the dugout with a fat lip, scowling at the Mexican youth, whose eye was beginning to puff and discolor. The Dodger captain cornered them both. "What the hell y'all doin' out there!? Both y'all got mouths -- somebody call for those kind! Willy B, you shoulda been hollerin' all the way! Then y'all got to tangle about it! I got a good mind...."

Willy B brushed him aside. "Hey, let's just get those runs back. Everybody makes an error now and then. I shoulda called it, Hey-Sue. Hey, you got a pretty good right! Shake?"

Hey-Sue didn't say much, but now he spoke. "Don't call me spic again, okay?" His black eyes glittered.

Willy B winced as he tried to grin past his swelling lip. "How about 'Tiger'? You pack a mean punch. I just didn't know you were man enough to throw it."

Charlie Perkins, the Mauler catcher, spoke as Blue Daddy stepped into the box. "I'll say one thing. You guys sure make the game int'restin' as hell!"

With two outs and nobody on, Longmile inserted Luke as a pinchhitter for Hey-Sue, for Third had assured him that he was fine and could at least play first. The Maulers had no clue as to the power or ability of the CF Kid, who had instructions from his coach to swing for the fences. Luke took two strikes and a ball before getting the pitch he wanted, and sent the sphere far over the centerfield fence. As the youngster trotted slowly past the shortstop, Potter remarked, "Thought you was s'posed to be sick, White Boy?!"

Luke choked slightly from the effort to reply while trotting. "No beer, Black Boy. Makes me strong!" he grinned.

The game ended at nine to eight, Maulers. There was one close play at first base in the ninth, when Red's throw was high, but the Mauler runner dodged Third's stretching body. "Thanks," the towhead grinned.

"Didn't wanta make that Mexican mad at ME!" the runner smiled.

TEAM *Barefoot Dodgers* RECORD   TEAM   RE

NO.	PLAYERS	B/A	POS/INN	1	2	3	4	5	6
1	Willy B	RF				1-3	F9		
	SUB. Brown Bro	RF	AVG						
	SUB.								
2	Jimmy Lee	1B							
	SUB. Sherman	2B	4						
	SUB.			E5	61	RBI			
3	Buzz	P	1B/4			F9		F9	
	SUB. II	1B	6						
	SUB.								
4	Hump	C			F8			E6	
	SUB.				RBI			RBI	
	SUB.								
5	Caleb	LF		6-4				F8	
	SUB.								
	SUB.								
6	Spider	SS		6-4-3				6-3	
	SUB.						RBI		
	SUB.								
7	Rafe	CF	P/4		5-3	3-4			
	SUB. Hay-Sue	CF	4						
	SUB.								
8	Junior	3B		F9		4-3	K		
	SUB. Luke		BN/5						
	SUB. Red	3B	PH/5						
9	Blue Daddy	2B			K				
	SUB. Wilbur ←	2B	P/6				2 RBI		
	SUB.								
	SUB.								
	SUB.								
	Coach - Longmile								
	SUB.								
	SUB.								

UMPIRE *Uncle Eb*

	1	2	3	4	5
R/H	4/3	3/2	1/1	1/0	/
LOB/ER	1/	1/	1/0	1/	/
E	E	E	E	E	E
B/P	B/P		B/P		

Chapter Twenty-Nine

Longmile's team meeting back at the hotel was short and to the point. "Okay, guys," he spoke matter-of-factly, "We can't lose another one. We kinda let that one get away from us today, but that's the way it goes sometimes. We didn't play sharp ball and we didn't get to play our best lineup. That wasn't our fault and we knew it was a fight we was gonna have to fight before we come up here.

"But we don't need to be fightin' amongst ourselves. Hey-Sue, Willy B, have y'all got everything outa your systems now? Y'all ready to play ball like the rest of the team?"

"Yessir," both youngsters replied at once, each holding a bag of ice to his face.

The coach grinned, "Actually, I figgered it'd come to that, sooner or later."

He rose and stretched. "Well, y'all relax and get a good night's sleep. See a movie -- there's a theater down the street. Get your mind off the game for a few hours and be rested when we hit the field tomorrow. Third, you doin' okay now? You gotta pitch against these guys."

"Yessir," the towhead responded. "I feel good; ready to throw."

"Aw right. You and Hump and Buzz hang around for a few minutes and let's talk about these Mauler batters. Resta you guys, outa here. Relax and get some rest. Let's win these last two games big!"

As the Dodgers filed out, Rafe nudged Blue Daddy. "Hey, man, let's find some music and kick back for awhile tonight. Whacha say?"

"Fine with me," the drummer replied. "Let's motivate on

down the street and see if we can find a juke joint."

The two Dodgers wandered for several blocks before they happened upon a night club from whence came the sounds of music they identified with. Entering the smokey atmosphere, Blue Daddy cocked one hand behind his ear. "Man, I can beat that drummer all hollow! And that guitar don't sound as good as yours by a long shot."

"Two beers," Rafe called as they stepped up to the bar. "And who's in charge of the music around this joint?"

The bartender served them the brew in bottles, and then pointed to a tall thin man who sat at a corner table by himself. "See Slim over there. He's the one sets up the bands. You guys play?"

"Hey, man," Rafe toasted his companion, "We're just the best!"

After an hour and several more beers at Slim's table, the two Brownspur youths had talked their way into performing while the rest of the band members took their scheduled break. It only took Blue and Rafe one number from their own repertoire to get the hang of borrowed instruments and unfamiliar acoustics. When the hired band finished their break, Slim was impressed enough to suggest "Let them jam with y'all for awhile, Danny." As the regular evening crowd began to fill the joint, the reception to the new musicians waxed enthusiastic, and like any performers, Rafe and Blue Daddy responded to the cheers and dancing. The band's regular drummer finally conceded gracefully to better talent, turned his sticks over to Blue, and asked a girl to dance. Slim came up with an extra guitar, and Rafe joined in.

Time flew, and the beer flowed freely. Along in the wee hours of the morning, the crowd began to break up, and Rafe realized what time it was. "Man, Longmile's gonnna kill us if he catches us sneaking back in this late!"

Slim pointed upstairs. "We got some extra pads up there. Why don't y'all bunk with us the rest of the night. We'll get you up tomorrow in time for your game."

"Aw, man, yeah!" the lead singer agreed. "Once the payin' customers leave, we really do some hot licks!"

Blue Daddy raised his eyebrows at Rafe. "Okay by me."

His companion nodded, "Sure. Pass me another brew."

NO.	PLAYERS	B/A	POS./INN	1	2	3	4	5	6
1	Willy B	RF				1-3	F9		
	SUB. Brown Bro	RF	PH/4						
	SUB.								
2	Jimmy Lee	1B							
	SUB. Sherman	2B	4	E30	61	RBI			
	SUB.								
3	Buzz	P	1B/4			F9		F7	
	SUB. III	1B	6						
	SUB.								
4	Hump	C			F8		E4		
	SUB.				RBI		RBI		
	SUB.								
5	Caleb	LF		6-4			F8		
	SUB.								
	SUB.								
6	Spider	SS		1-43		6-3			
	SUB.					RBI			
	SUB.								
7	Rafe	CF	P/4		5-3	3-4			
	SUB. Hay-Sue	CF	4						
	SUB.								
8	Junior	3B		F9	4-3	K			
	SUB. Luke		PH/5						
	SUB. Red	3B	PR/5						
9	Blue Paddy	2B		K					
	SUB. Wilbur	4th	2B P/6			2 RBI			
	SUB.								
	SUB.								
	SUB.								
Coach - Longmile									
	SUB.								
	SUB.								

UMPIRE	Uncle Eb

	1	2	3	4	5	6
R / H	4 / 3	3 / 2	1 / 1	1 / 0		
LOB / ER	/	/	/	/	/	/
E						
B/p						

Chapter Thirty

"Where's Rafe and Blue Daddy?" Longmile demanded as the team boarded the bus at ten o'clock for transport to the park.

"I ain't seen 'em this mornin'," Buzz noted. "Anybody seen 'em?" There were head shakes and shrugs. He stepped to the house phone and dialed the missing players' room number. There was no answer. "Brown Brother, run upstairs and beat on their door. They must be still asleep," he directed in disgust.

The youngster soon reappeared. "I even got the maid to open their room. Nobody's there, and it don't look like their beds been slept in."

Longmile turned to Mr. Leroy, who was having the same thought: "Reckon somethin's happened to 'em?"

The Brownspur owner took charge. "I don't know, but I'll find out. Uncle Eb, s'pose you stay with me and we'll run 'em down, wherever they are. Longmile, y'all go on to the ballpark and get loose. They prob'ly just slept late and ran out for a quick hamburger or somethin'. We'll bring 'em on when we locate 'em. Y'all kick tail until we get there!"

As the Barefoot Dodgers entered the bus, Longmile took Mr. Leroy aside. "You gotta get 'em back before game time, or we won't have enough to play ball....Unless...unless I start Luke."

"If we ain't back, you'll have to play him. Just everybody keep an eye on the boy, okay?"

"Mr. Leroy, if you ain't there, I don't wanta play Luke. He ain't gonna hold up in this type situation. He's gonna go balls to the wall if it means winnin' or losin' and if he gets too hot or has a coughin' spell, it could might near kill 'im. I can't take that kind of responsibility. Nossir!"

Leroy Alexander looked upward, past the tall buildings, past the clouds, past the shining sun. He took a deep breath and turned back to the coach. "Longmile, they told us a long time ago that Luke would be lucky to get old enough for a driver's license. He's never gotten to play in a regular baseball game before, much less a National Championship Series. Chances are that he'll never get another opportunity to do so, just like chances are he'll never get to graduate from high school. If you need him, play him."

"Nossir. Not me. I'll stay here and wait for Blue and Rafe, or else, let's just leave Uncle Eb to bring 'em. If anybody's gonna play Luke, I'd rather it was you."

"You know as well as I do that those two boys might be down at the jail or down at the morgue or somewhere in between. I'm responsible for Rafe and Blue, and if they're in trouble, I'm the only one can get 'em out -- if they can be got out. Shoot, the first place I got to call after the police, is the hospitals. Maybe they got mugged or somethin'. Point is, I've got to stay and find them, 'cause no one else can handle it if there's been some kind of trouble. You agree with that, don't you?"

"Yessir. But I'd rather forfeit the game, or at least ask for a postponement, than play Luke."

"Longmile, lemme tell you somethin'. That boy will never get a chance to play baseball unless it's now, and unless you're coachin' him. If he wants to play, I want him to. He's got guts, we all know that. Tell Buzz and Third to watch out for him. Nail his foot to the base, like you threatened to do." The father swallowed hard. "Old friend, Luke's never had the chances Third has, or most of these kids; and he ain't got many more years of chances left. If the Barefoot Dodgers were to forfeit this series because you wouldn't play Luke, it would break his heart. It'd hurt him a helluva lot more than playin' would, I believe. Give him a chance to be a real part of the team. All the boys deserve that. If Rafe and Blue are dead, hurt, or in jail, you ain't got but nine players left. Don't put Luke in the position of lettin' the rest of his team down -- 'cause this is HIS team, too, Longmile -- the only time he's ever really been on a sure 'nuff team in his life!" He winked away a tear. "And probably the last time."

The two men stood silently for a moment, one staring at the sidewalk, one gazing Heavenward again, waiting for an answer. Finally the black man nodded, slowly at first, then more positively. He looked toward the bus where his players waited, then back at the sidewalk. He scuffed his shoe along a crack in the cement, then dug at the corner of one eye with a fist before speaking to his white companion.

"Yessir," the coach said softly. He put his arm around his employer's shoulders. "I'll start our boy if you don't get Rafe or Blue back by game time."

"Thanks. Take care of all our boys, Coach. Good luck."

Turning to the elderly man, Mr. Leroy motioned toward the hotel. "C'mon, Uncle Eb. Let's start callin'. I'll get the police, and you go to work on the hospitals. I just hope they're okay."

The Barefoot Dodgers' bus pulled away from the curb as the two men, black and white, walked into the hotel.

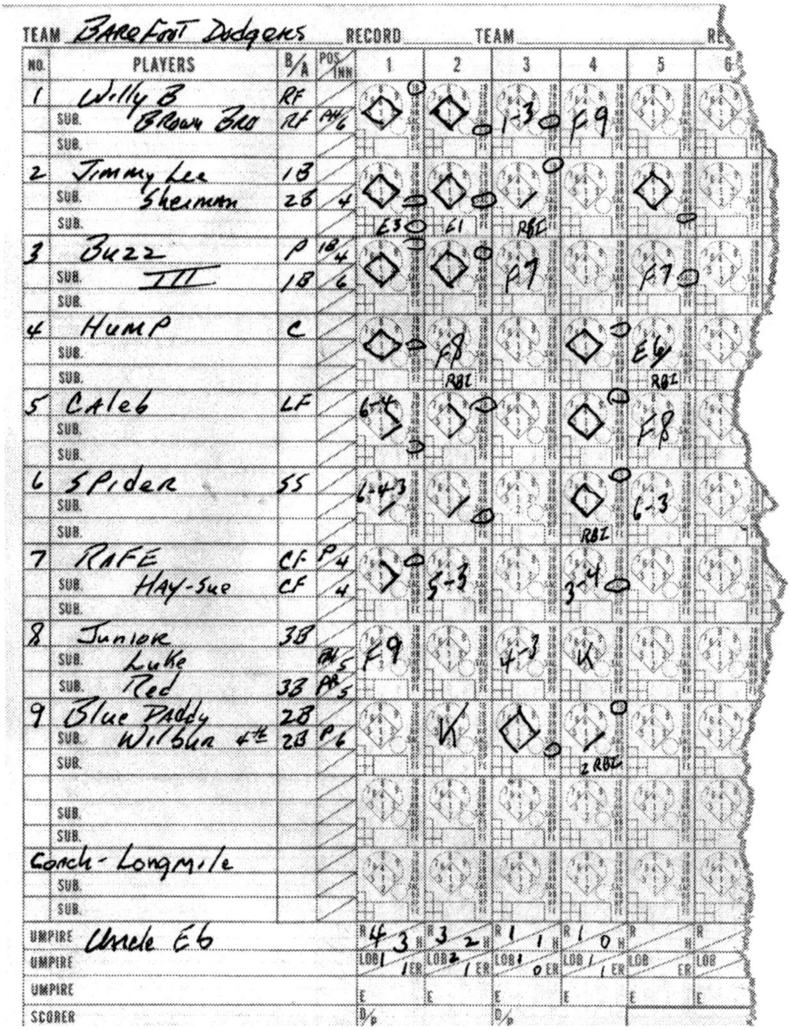

TEAM Barefoot Dodgers RECORD TEAM

NO.	PLAYERS	B/A	POS/INN	1	2	3	4	5	6
1	Willy B	RF		◇	◇	1-3	F9		
	SUB. Brown Bro	RF	PH/6						
2	Jimmy Lee	1B		◇ E3	◇ E1	/ RBI		◇	
	SUB. Sherman	2B	4						
3	Buzz	P	1B/4	◇	◇	F7		F7	
	SUB. III	1B	6						
4	Hump	C		◇	F8 RBI		◇	E6 RBI	
5	Caleb	LF		6-4			◇	F8	
6	Spider	SS		6-4-3			◇ RBI	6-3	
7	Rafe	CF	P/4		5-3		3-4		
	SUB. Hay-Sue	CF	4						
8	Junior	3B		F9		4-3	K		
	SUB. Luke		PH/5						
	SUB. Red	3B	PR/5						
9	Blue Daddy	2B			K	◇	/ 2 RBI		
	SUB. Wilbur 4th	2B	P/6						
	Coach - Longmile								
UMPIRE	Uncle E6			R 4 H 3	R 3 H 2	R 1 H 1	R 1 H 0		
UMPIRE				LOB 1 ER 1	LOB 2 ER 1	LOB 1 ER 0	LOB 1 ER 1		
UMPIRE									
SCORER									

Chapter Thirty-One

"No way!" John Henry Vester exclaimed. "Either we play it now, or you walk away from it. Rules say the games start at one each day, and the only reason for postponement is rain, weather, or an act of God. Hey, I'd like to get a postponement on that first game, remember? We'd be gone home by now, hadn't been for that freak home run pop-up! Play or forfeit, Longmile!"

"Dad blame it! John Henry, if you had somethin' to do with my two players bein' gone, I'll...."

"Hold on," the IAL president interjected. "Don't go accusin' him without evidence. I hope nothin's happened to your guys, Coach, and we'll get their descriptions on the radio and teevee. But, technically, John Henry's right. You gotta play."

"Here's my line-up," growled the Brownspur coach, and walked away to his dugout.

Luke had just returned from the pressbox telephone where, at Longmile's instructions, he had called the hotel again. "No sign of 'em yet, Coach. Daddy says all they know is, they ain't in jail anywhere in St. Louis, they're not in the city morgue, and none of the hospitals say they've got anybody by their names. He and Uncle Eb are fixin' to go down the streets lookin', and have got several cop cars cruisin' around. Daddy says 'Good luck!'"

"Okay, guys, here's the way we got to play it. Luke, you're on first, and I don't want you movin' three feet...."

"Coach, we been talkin' it over," the CF Kid interrupted respectfully. "With Third pitchin' -- and Hump says his sidearm is really movin' good warmin' up -- we all know they're gonna hit most everything into the ground or pop it up. Buzz is ten times a better first baseman than I am. Put me out in center, so we'll have the strongest infield, 'cause that's where everything's goin'. I promise I won't run after anything very far."

"Caleb and I will fudge over toward center and watch after Luke," Willy B offered. The left fielder nodded.

"Makes sense," Buzz told his coach. "If Luke promises to take it easy, he'd prob'ly have to move around less in center, at least as long as Third keeps 'em low. If he starts gettin' 'em up, well, we can always switch up."

Third agreed. "I'm throwin' good, Longmile. Ask Hump." That worthy nodded.

Finally the coach shrugged, in the face of team logic. "Okay. But Luke, dammit, don't you run! And at bat, it's the same rule: hit for the fences, understand?"

The CF Kid grinned. "Home runs all day long! Just hope my big brother can shut down their bats."

Which Third did completely for six innings. The towhead was brilliant on the mound, his curve breaking sharp, his change-up and knuckler dancing tantilizingly out in front of the Mauler batters. Third didn't strike a single batter out, but to only one hitter did he throw more than three pitches, when Treetop fouled off four in a row before Hump got under one.

The problem was, from the Barefoot Dodger viewpoint, that Spike was almost as perfect on the Mauler mound. Through six innings, there was only one baserunner for either side, when Spider bunted for a single but died on first when Caleb whiffed on three pitches. It was one of the fastest games Longmile had ever participated in, on the exact day when he wanted a game to drag on, hoping his missing players would show up. Luke called back to the hotel in the fourth, but there was no word at all.

In the seventh, both pitchers tired a little. Hump got hold of Spike's fastball and drilled it into the gap in right for a double, was sacrificed to third, and tagged up to score on Luke's towering fly to left. This only tied the score, however, for the

Mauler leadoff had drag bunted safely, stolen second -- though both Longmile and Hey-Sue argued the call, was safe at third on a fielder's choice -- though Red argued that call valiantly ("Red always argues his calls," Spider grinned at the exasperated ump), and came home on the first ball hit out of the infield, a dying quail that Willy B made a diving catch on, but couldn't throw in time to beat the runner.

Both teams loaded the bases in the eighth, but neither scored. Longmile visited the mound anxiously to confer with his infielders. "Third, you want me to switch you and Buzz? Or else, Buzz, I might move you to center. Those last two guys got good wood to Caleb and Willy B. How you feel, Third?"

The towhead considered. "I think they're just gettin' used to my stuff. What about it, Hump? Think Buzz might take over?"

The catcher shook his head. "I wish Rafe was here, durnit! You could bring his speed in and blow 'em out quick. Pop, lemme stick with Third and pitch this next guy high and tight to start out with. He's still got good control. We'll shake the hitter up, move him back in the box, and maybe he'll top that outside curve."

The strategy worked perfectly, though Coach Vester angrily protested that the "white boy was throwin' at my batter!" Buzz gobbled up a weak grounder, tagged the batter headed to first, and fired home to Hump, who blocked the plate and got the out to double up the Maulers. There was a confrontation between the runner and the Dodger catcher, the two coaches, and the umpire, that threatened a brawl after the play, but the IAL officials had learned their lesson early, and were between the combatants before blows were actually passed. Luke and Casey Potter, the former running in from center, calmed the teams down, mindful of the pledges they had made to each other in the earlier game.

In the top of the ninth, Luke had a coughing spell that necessitated the IAL doctor's attention, but there was oxygen available, and the CF Kid was able to return to the field. Once more, Longmile huddled with his players to consider shifting Luke to first, but he couldn't argue with the logic, "Coach, I couldn't have made that double play Buzz made. Leave him in the infield. I ain't had a fly all day."

But he had one that inning. With two out, Casey Potter got ahold of one of Third's change-ups. It was obviously not going out of the park, but it was deep to center, perhaps off the wall. Luke never hesitated. He turned his back to the ball and sprinted for the fence, in spite of "Luke, No!" yells from his brother, Buzz, Longmile, and Brown Brother. Willy B and Caleb, already fudged over to protect him most of the game, converged, both yelling "I got it!" even though they knew they didn't. Their yells were simply to try to slow their comrade. Even Casey slowed on the basepaths momentarily at the shouting, until his own coach screamed, "Run, dammit!"

Luke's stride broke ten steps before the wall, but it was obvious that he could not have reached this ball, for all his efforts. It hit high on the wall and ricocheted left, and Caleb, who had been the victim of such a bad bounce the game before, was the lucky recipient of a good one this time. The ball hit his glove and he wheeled to fire a perfect throw to Red Wood, who made the tag, though being bowled over by the sliding Mauler captain. Third grabbed Red, shouting, "It was a clean slide! Clean slide!" to avert his teammate's temper. Willy B and Caleb bent over Luke, who was coughing up gobs of phlegm in center.

They helped the CF Kid back to the bench, where the doctor administered more oxygen. Third, having calmed Red with Hump and Spider's help, anxiously attended his younger brother. "Let's get some Gatorade in him," he told Buzz. Longmile huddled with the umpire.

"I got a problem. This kid's s'posed to bat second this inning,

Ump. You can see he ain't up to it. Lemme hit somebody else for him, please!"

John Henry Vester was right beside him, arguing, "You ain't got nobody to pinchhit, Coach, and if you bring somebody in out of order, he's out. You wanta forfeit?"

"Dammit, John Henry, cut me some slack!" the Dodger coach exclaimed, raising his voice. The players close enough to hear edged closer, expecting another fight between coaches. The IAL president advanced onto the field, just as Longmile turned away in disgust.

"Coach, we just got a call! They've found your players, and are on the way with them," he declared.

"Ump, I need a delay until they get here," the Dodger coach pleaded.

"Only an act of God, or weather, can get you a delay," Vester interjected. "Batter up, Ump, or I'm gonna ask for a forfeit." The umpire looked at the president for help, but he just shrugged. Players from both teams had by now gathered around the group. "Play or lose," Vester repeated.

The youngsters parted for Brown Brother and Luke, the latter still hawking and leaning on his friend. "I can...hold a bat... Longmile." There was the ghost of a smile on the lips of the CF Kid. "Shoot, I'll...park...(a-huuuucck, spit)...one if Spike...can get it over!"

The umpire looked at John Henry Vester in disgust. "Okay, let's play ball, folks!"

Longmile leaned to Buzz, who was to lead off the ninth. "Take all the time you can. Stall. Foul off pitches. Argue with the calls. Stall, you hear?" The captain nodded.

Coach Vester finally emerged from the dugout to protest Buzz's tactics: stepping out of the box before the pitch, calling time to retie his shoes, knocking dirt from his cleats endlessly, talking with the umpire about the calls. The ump had to agree. "Take your bat, son." Buzz finally flied to center, after delaying nearly ten minutes. Still no sign of Rafe and Blue Daddy, but it was nearly a twenty-minute drive from the hotel.

Luke was breathing easier when he stepped to the plate and took his practice swings. The fluid and oxygen had revived him to some extent, and Buzz's delay had given him time to relax and control his coughing. Casey Potter called time to talk to his pitcher. "Blow three by 'im, Spike. This guy don't need to be up there long. But don't groove one; he's gotten good wood on everything today." Spike nodded.

Luke stood in the box and took two strikes without moving his bat off his shoulders. "Now you ready," Brown Brother called from the dugout, where Longmile was watching the runway for Mr. Leroy, Uncle Eb, Rafe, and Blue Daddy. Just as Spike went into his windup, he saw his players loping toward the gate. "Aw right!" he exclaimed, turning to call for a time out.

But Luke swung -- for the fences, as instructed. He got all of a good fastball, and everyone in the park knew that it was gone when the bat cracked. Spike kicked at the mound, and the outfielders never moved, the closest one simply raising his head to watch the sphere leave the park. The CF Kid pounded his fist into his palm, dropped his bat, and began his trot around the bases. He was almost to second when the coughing fit hit him.

At first, the boy stooped, hands on knees, and coughed, hawked, and spit. His face turned redder, and he dropped to his knees. The Barefoot Dodgers, joined now by a sheepish Blue and Rafe, as well as Uncle Eb and Mr. Leroy, exited the dugout, their cheers quieted. Longmile stepped toward the baseline, to be halted by the shout of the Mauler coach. "Ump, he crosses that line, and the run don't count. If the runner can't make it around, it ain't a homer!"

Longmile rushed the umpire. "C'mon, Ump! You can see what kinda shape he's in. My other players just got here. Lemme put a pinch runner in."

Now the Mauler dugout was emptying behind their coach. Vester was at the umpire's side. "No substitutes during a play, and this play ain't over until that kid either crosses the plate or don't cross it and you call 'im out for delay! And if a man on their team goes onto the field before that, he's out! You know the rules!"

The IAL president was now on the field, with the attorney. Mr. Leroy, Third, Buzz, and Brown Brother were standing at the baseline, watching Luke and clearly about to go to his aid. The Mauler coach screamed, "Any of their guys help 'im, it's an out, Ump. He's gotta do it himself!"

Longmile roared in frustration, "Well then, you sonuvabitch, to hell with the damn ball game!" and wheeled to go to his stricken player. He was stopped by a call from the field.

"Wait!" yelled Casey Potter, over the din. Even the fans in the stands quieted at his command. "What if one of our team helps him, Ump?"

"Rules just say you can't interfere with the runner, Short," the third base umpire replied.

Casey Potter dropped his glove at deep short and walked toward the kneeling Barefoot Dodger. With one arm around Luke's waist, and the other holding his opponent's arm across his own shoulders, he helped the CF Kid to stand. "Be sure you don't miss steppin' on second base, White Boy," he directed.

The Mauler captain was nearly to third base with his burden when his coach bellowed, "What the hell you doin', Casey?! Put that white boy down!" Suddenly there was a strong arm across his own shoulders, and laid there none too gently.

"Hush up, Coach!" Treetop ordered.

The Mauler third baseman also dropped his glove as Casey and Luke approached his bag, and reached for the other arm. "There ya go, just step on the base," he said as the three made the turn toward home.

"LUKE, LUKE, LUKE, LUKE!" began the Dodger chant as the trio came down the third base line, and the fans picked up the chant. Mr. Leroy gripped Third's arm. Longmile stood at the plate, hands outstretched. Uncle Eb knelt in obvious prayer, and the IAL president patted the old man's shoulder. John Henry Vester watched in openmouthed disbelief as his shortstop and third baseman carried Luke home, followed in file by his other fielders. Just short of the plate, Casey Potter stopped, as the "LUKE, LUKE, LUKE!" noise rolled over them like ocean waves.

"You make it from here, White Boy?" he smiled. His burden hawked, spit, wiped his mouth feebly, and coughed. "Yeah," he managed. "Thanks." The CF Kid took two wobbly steps onto home plate and fell into his coach's arms as the umpire signaled "Safe!" The IAL doctor was there with oxygen, and a syringe.

The crowd stood, stomping their feet in time to the chant, "LUKE, LUKE, LUKE, LUKE!" At the edge of the Barefoot Dodger dugout, the CF Kid stopped to raise his arms to the fans. He didn't have to depend on his own muscles. Buzz held one hand high as Casey Potter raised the other. Third turned to his tearful father. "He's gonna be all right, Daddy, if he can think about the stands!"

Chapter Thirty-Two

Longmile had method in his madness when he sent Luke out with the line-up for the final game of the IAL National Championship Series. "I don't wanta see that ugly John Henry's mug today, Luke; you feel like takin' the sheet over?"

A pale and weak, but recovering, CF Kid grinned. "Sure, Coach. You positive you don't want me in center today?"

As the crowd recognized the hero from the day before, they began their chant, "LUKE, LUKE, LUKE, LUKE!" Third noticed that it was almost like a cadence, and that his younger brother was marching smartly to it as he started back toward the dugout. Suddenly, the CF Kid skipped, and changed feet, throwing the crowd off timing. The stands broke into laughter as Luke tipped his cap before entering the dugout. "Ham!" Third kidded, punching his shoulder.

"Careful, son. You might need another homer outa that."

"Nah," Spider replied. "Rafe and Blue gonna provide the punch today. Take a break, Luke."

"Okay, boys," Longmile addressed them simply. "This is it. Let's go get 'em."

Willy B pounced on Treetop Smiley's first pitch, lining it into the gap in right, and stretched it to a triple. Spider laid down a perfect bunt with the runner going, and though the Mauler third sacker was expecting a bunt, he still couldn't make the play at home. The Dodgers led one to nothing after two pitches.

Which was enough of a lead for Buzz for four innings, when Charlie Perkins rifled a shot back through the box that bounced off the pitcher's shin. Longmile walked out as his captain hopped and limped around the mound. After examining the injury himself, he beckoned for the IAL doctor, who said nothing was broken. However, it was obvious after a few practice pitches that Buzz was going to be favoring the leg for a while, anyway. Rafe was brought in from center field to pitch.

"You ready to do somethin' today, since you had a day off yesterday to rest up?" the coach asked sarcastically.

"Yessir," his player responded remorsefully. After watching him warm up, Longmile was satisfied that the day off might have helped Rafe. At least, his control was good to start off.

The Maulers had learned to respect Rafe's pickoff move, and Perkins wasn't a speedster anyway. Buzz, taking over at first while Third went to center, didn't even bother to hold the runner. Rafe struck out one batter, and the second hit a long fly down the line that Caleb camped under, the runner tagging and advancing after the catch. The next Mauler foul-tipped a third strike that Hump held onto.

In the sixth, the Dodgers added an insurance run when Blue was safe on an error by the second baseman, was sacrified to second, and took third on a passed ball that Charlie Perkins blocked, but couldn't find the handle on. Red Wood flied to right to bring him home.

In the seventh, Treetop got all of one of Rafe's fastballs, and sent it into the seats in left. The Dodger hurler lost control momentarily, walking one man and hitting another, before the leadoff hitter, who had been a thorn in the Dodgers' side the whole series, caught Red playing back and bunted safely. The third sacker walked the ball to the mound to apologize to Rafe. "Sorry, man; I was playin' 'em to hit and run, lookin' for a double play."

Rafe bore down and struck the next man out, then kept his pitches down and away from Casey Potter, who finally grounded weakly to Blue Daddy, who turned Red's expected double play to end the Mauler threat.

The teams traded runs in the eighth, Caleb homering for the Dodgers, and Perkins tripling down the right field line and coming home on a grounder behind second that Spider speared but had to go to Buzz on. Longmile went to the mound. "What about it, Rafe? Think we ought to go with Third's junk behind you?"

His pitcher took a deep breath. "It's worked before, coach. They're beginnin' to read me. What about it, Hump?"

The catcher nodded, "You've thrown pretty good, Rafe. Let's see if Third can shut 'em down. He didn't use too many pitches yesterday." Longmile waved the towhead in from center.

"Good game, Rafe," Third slapped the righty on the rear. He needed four pitches to get out of the inning, for the Maulers were so used to Rafe's speed, as Longmile had predicted.

In the Mauler ninth, John Henry Vester rallied his team. "Now or never, guys. You got to wait on this white boy's junk! Fudge up in the box and wait on those slow curves. Let's get at least one run, to stay alive."

The Mauler leadoff followed his coach's instructions, fouling off three pitches before completely surprising the Dodger infield with a two-strike drag bunt. "Caught me flatfooted," Buzz said ruefully as he handed the ball into Third's glove.

"Let's double 'im up," his pitcher encouraged.

Not to be. Hump lost the handle momentarily on a knuckleball, and the runner was going. Blue Daddy's tag was nowhere near on time. The stands began to get excited, and the Mauler dugout turned their caps around and started clapping. Coach Vester conferred with his batter. "Hang in there and don't go fishin' on those change-ups and knucklers. Get a rap!"

A lefthander usually has a pretty good move to first, but seldom to second, and the Mauler coach knew that. The batter squared around to fake a bunt, blocking Hump's move on the next pitch, and the runner was going. Red Wood jumped from the flashing cleats, conceding the bag as Hump faked the throw. The tying run was ninety feet away, with no outs. "Bear down, Third," Luke yelled, but could hardly be heard for the crowd.

The Dodger southpaw was upset, and did something Third almost never did: he walked the batter. With runners at the corners, Buzz called time and motioned the infielders toward the mound. "Suck it up, guys. Let's play to cut the run off, okay? Third, this guy can hit. You all right? Want me or Rafe to come back in?"

"Nah, I'm okay. Just got a little rattled. Let's cut 'im down, guys! Hump, you gotta block the plate, now."

"I can hack that. Y'all just throw straight."

Third pitched carefully to the hitter, while also having to hold the runner on at first. Coach Vester flashed the hit and run sign on the third pitch, and the batter went after a curve on the outside corner, with the runners moving. "Go!" yelled the Mauler coach, as the bat cracked. It was a screaming shoetop liner to first base, and Buzz had broken toward the hole as the runner left. The Dodger captain had to reverse and dive with all his length to make a play. The ball smacked into his glove just before the sphere touched the ground, and Buzz's momentum carried him across first in a roll. He heard the first base umpire cry "Out!" as he rolled to his knees to throw to Hump. He realized he had just pulled off a double play, and could see that the runner was going to hit the Dodger catcher. He faked a throw and lunged to his feet, yelling at the first base umpire, "Ump, I caught that ball in the air!" The man in blue yelled back, "I know, son!" as Buzz charged the plate, which was the center of action.

The runner had hit Hump hard enough to jar loose the expected throw, and now was frantically reaching with one hand for home, while the Dodger catcher rolled over clutching a cleat-sliced thigh. "Safe! Safe!" screamed the Mauler coach as the runner's hand pounded the plate. Coach, runner, and home ump all hovered over the injured catcher. "The ball! Where's the ball? Did he hold onto it?"

Buzz Waterman sprinted up, followed closely by the first base umpire. He smiled proudly as he held up the white baseball in his ungloved hand. "Here t'is," he declared, and touched the Mauler runner with the ball.

"Yer out!" bellowed the first base ump. "Triple play! He caught the line drive, doubled the runner off first, and this runner failed to tag up at third! He's out! Game's over!"

"Hot damn!" Uncle Eb exclaimed, who had taken it all in. "An unassisted triple play! I never seen that before!"

"Ain't no need to cuss," Hey-Sue grinned.

And then the stands went wild.

Luke Alexander approached the Mauler captain with his hand extended. "Good game, good series, Casey. Thanks for everything you did for me and us."

The shortstop put his arm around the CF Kid's shoulders. "Hey, some teams are okay to lose to! Great series, White Boy."

TEAM *Barefoot Dodgers* RECORD_____ TEAM _____

NO.	PLAYERS	B/A	POS/INN	1	2	3	4	5	6
1	Willy B	RF				1-3	F9		
	SUB. Brown Bro	RF	AVG						
	SUB.								
2	Jimmy Lee	1B							
	SUB. Sherman	2B	4	ESO	61	RBI			
	SUB.								
3	Buzz	P 1B/4				F9		F9	
	SUB. II	1B	6						
	SUB.								
4	Hump	C			F8			E6	
	SUB.					RBI		RBI	
	SUB.								
5	Caleb	LF		6-4				F8	
	SUB.								
	SUB.								
6	Spider	SS		6-4-3				6-3	
	SUB.						RBI		
	SUB.								
7	Rafe	CF P4			5-3	3-4			
	SUB. Hay-Sue	CF	4						
	SUB.								
8	Junior	3B		F9		4-3	K		
	SUB. Luke		BA/5						
	SUB. Red	3B	PA/5						
9	Blue Daddy	2B			K				
	SUB. Wilbur 4th	2B	P6				2 RBI		
	SUB.								
	SUB.								
	SUB.								
	Coach - Longmile								
	SUB.								
	SUB.								
UMPIRE Uncle Eb				R 4 3	R 3 2	R 1 1	R 1 0	R	
UMPIRE				LOB 1	LOB 2	LOB 1	LOB 1	LOB	
UMPIRE				E	E	E	E	E
SCORER				B/P	B/P			

182   *The Barefoot Dodgers*

Epilogue

Buzz Waterman knocked on the plantation office door, surprising Mr. Leroy, who had apparently been lost in thought. "Hey, Buzz!" the plantation owner exclaimed. "I didn't know anyone was around on Sunday afternoon. Good to see you!"

"Mr. Leroy, I didn't know. We were playin' two series on the west coast, and the message from Longmile took three days to catch up to me. I'm sorry."

"Aw, man, I just 'preciate you comin' now! You didn't really need to. We got your telegram the day after the funeral. Thanks for thinkin' of us when you're in the middle of a pennant race. Speakin' of that, how'd you get away now?"

"Told 'em I'd had a death in the family. Felt like that, too. Hope you don't mind me sayin' that."

The older man fumbled in his desk drawer and flipped the key to the drink machine to his companion. His voice seemed to break a little as he said, "Why don't you get a couple of drinks?" When Buzz returned, there was a pint bottle of clear liquid in the farmer's hand. "Late enough in the afternoon for you?"

"That Uncle Eb's?" the pitcher grinned.

"He still claims his cousin makes it. Whatever, it ain't killed him yet." Mr. Leroy poured a sample into both drink bottles.

Both men took their time tasting the mixture, Buzz drawing his top lip back off his teeth and inhaling noticibly afterward.

"Was it...bad?" he finally asked.

"Well...yeah. He fought it all the way. We..." his voice broke, and Mr. Leroy took another swig before continuing. "We had to finally take him off the respirator. There just wasn't any hope and he was all used up, Buzz." The man seemed like he was seeking justification.

"He beat the odds for a helluva lot longer than we ever figured, Mr. Leroy. And, by God, sir, he got all the goody he could out of life! If you don't mind me sayin' so."

"He did," the father agreed.

They drank in companionable silence for a while, until Buzz stood to rub the huge trophy on the shelf over the desk. "That was one helluva summer," he mused.

"Sure was. I wouldn't take a pretty for havin' lived it, and havin' my sons live it. A helluva summer," the white man declared, and mock-toasted the pitcher. "And your big break."

"No kiddin'! I'da never dreamed...well, that's all it was, just a dream. Who'da ever thought...."

"Big leagues for Buzz! Only one year of minor league ball. Not many folks can make the jump that quick, son. Eighteen game winner last year, and prob'ly twenty this year, especially if y'all win the pennant and get into the Series. We're proud of you, Buzz."

"I got lucky, Mr. Leroy. Whatever happened to Spider? I ain't heard from him in two years."

"Got a good field, no hit, reputation in AA ball. He ended up gettin' married and is coachin' for a junior college out in Texas somewhere. I've got his address in my file. Last I saw 'im, he'd gained twenty pounds. He had a good run at it, and seems happy coachin'."

"Good. I see Blue Daddy nearly every time we play in New York. He's hittin' the big time with that band. Wish Rafe had been able to stick to it."

"Yeah. His daddy told me last week he was in another drug rehab program somewhere in the mid-west. Maybe even St. Louis?"

"I heard. Where's Third now?"

"He went back to Ole Miss after the funeral. You know, they

red-shirted him when he tore his knee up, and he pitched another year of college ball, but somehow his sidearm never really was sharp after the operations. He's gettin' his degree in pre-med next spring. Wish he was still here to see you. He keeps up with all your stats. You ain't got a bigger fan."

Buzz ducked his head modestly. "Brown Brother used to keep me up to date, but he's discovered girls this past couple years. He and Luke wrote regular up until then. He said Hump and Red went off to Alaska?"

Mr. Leroy nodded. "You know, they were always good with mechanical things. They went to the Vo-Tech School, took some weldin' course, and last time Longmile heard from Hump, they were makin' an ungodly amount of money! And cold, too," he grinned.

"Caleb still here on the place?"

"Sure. He's runnin' the gin for me now. Hey-Sue's family left that next year, and I've lost track of them. I figure Caleb will be here forever, just like his old daddy."

"Mr. Leroy, how old is Uncle Eb?"

"Got to be in his nineties now. He was in his seventies when he fathered Caleb. He'll make a hundred, I'd bet. Still talks about that summer."

"Y'all don't have a team still, Brown Brother said."

"Uh-uh. The gov'ment more or less outlawed sharecroppin' two years after that. We went from havin' forty-five families to eight on Brownspur, and there's only five left now. Doin' it all with tractors and mechanical pickers. But Buzz, it ain't much fun anymore. Takin' the people out of farmin' took the pleasure out of it. It's different."

"Where'd everybody go?"

"Town at first, where the gov'ment threw up some rent-free housin'. There's not any industry around for jobs, so then the gov'ment had to put everybody on food stamps and welfare. Lordee, there's Medicare, Medicaid, ADC, so much from so many programs. It's almost busted the local and state economies. Nobody's got gardens, or cows, or hogs, or chickens, or roastin' ear patches. Things have really changed, Buzz. You left at a good time."

"Yessir, that's what Daddy says. Longmile's still here, though."

"My foreman. Couldn't run the place without him. I tried to get him to take that trophy to keep, but he wouldn't hear of it. Said it belonged down here at the office after Luke died.... Say, would you take it, Buzz? You were captain."

The former Barefoot Dodger blinked in surprise. "Why... I couldn't do that, Mr. Leroy. It was your team. You paid for everything, and Luke and Third were your boys....Nossir, I wouldn't feel right takin' that away from Brownspur."

"You were all my boys, Buzz; leastways, I felt thataway. Have you got a place to put that -- maybe next to your future MVP and Cy Young Awards?"

"Mr. Leroy, I couldn't," the major league pitcher seemed strangely overwhelmed. "That was Luke's, everybody knew that."

"Luke's gone now, Buzz. He's gone, and Willy B's dead too, after his wreck last year. Third was the last besides you to still be playin' baseball, and he's through now. You're the only active player left from the Barefoot Dodgers, the International Amateur League Champions. In the spirit of that team, won't you take this trophy for luck?"

"For luck...and Luke. Mr. Leroy, I don't know what to say. I'll take it, if you'll give it. That was my big chance, and I'll never forget that summer, nor those guys. Nor Brownspur. Yessir." He stood to lift the trophy almost reverently. "I'll take it, and be proud to show it off. Thank you, sir."

The Brownspur owner reached to clasp the pitcher's hand. "Thank you, Buzz. God be with you!"

Mr. Leroy rummaged back in the drawer and held out the key to the drink machine. "Still some of Cuz's brew here. Get us another cold drink while I hold your trophy one last time?"

"My pleasure," grinned Buzz Waterman.

The Barefoot Dodgers

Acknowledgements

I would be remiss in not thanking several folks for making The Barefoot Dodgers possible. Let's start where it all – and I do mean ALL – begins: with God. As I described in the Foreword, I believe this'n was given to me to write by the Creator. Why me, Lord? On the other hand, why not me? I was there.

I'd have to thank the late Bud Granger, who helped me flesh out the story after I had written the beginning and end; and Jessie Ford, for coming through with the real names, then literally putting his best feet forward; and Jessie's Daddy, Pete, for providing feet for this, and his memories of those days.

Of course, thanks to Betsy, to whom I have been wed for 42 years thus far, and who provided the hospitality for countless baseball players and kids, plus being my inspiration, as well as for her guidance for actually putting this book together.

For the mechanics, thanks to Mark Weilenman, and I need to go into that in depth.

Jesse Heath and I led the music on Central Mississippi Emmaus Walk # 75, in April of 2006, having been assigned that task by Mark, who was the Lay Leader of that men's retreat. Some of the members of that Team then formed a Tuesday morning Prayer and Share Group, and one morning, my prayer request was for help in getting The Barefoot Dodgers into the proper computer format.

Mark said, "I have those programs on my computer. I can do this for you." Though there was an initial problem in converting my disk, Mark put this story into book form, then laid out the cover, with advice from Betsy.

This whole experience has been kind of a God Thing! Thanks to Him for providing His people to publish The Barefoot Dodgers.

The Barefoot Dodgers

Printed in the United States
127232LV00002B/28-51/A